8/18

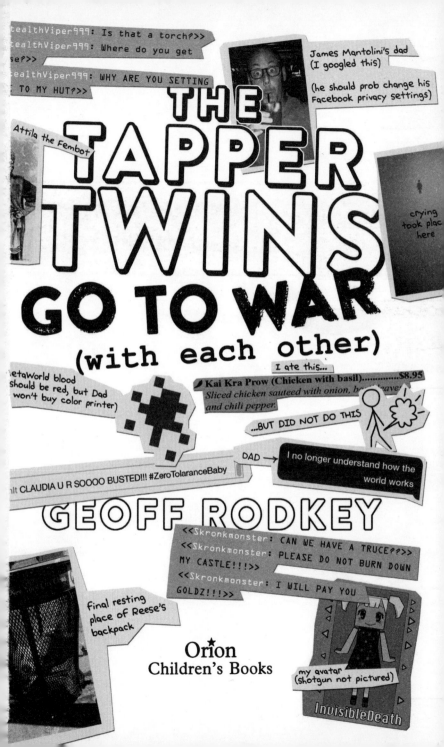

Look out for. . .

THE TAPPER TWINS
TEAR UP NEW YORK

(coming soon)

First published in Great Britain 2015
by Orion Children's Books
an imprint of Hachette Children's Group
and published by Hodder and Stoughton Limited

Orion House
5 Upper St Martin's Lane
London WC2 9EA
An Hachette UK Company

1 3 5 7 9 10 8 6 4 2

Printed in Great Britain by Clays Ltd, St Ives plc

978 1 4440 1497 6

www.orionchildrensbooks.co.uk

CONTENTS

PROLOGUE
(i.e., the very, very beginning)

CLAUDIA

Wars are terrible things. I know this because I've read about a lot of them on Wikipedia.

And also because I was just in one. It was me against my brother, Reese.

That might not sound like a war to you. Trust me. It was. In fact, it was a lot like other famous wars I've read about on Wikipedia.

Just like World War II, it involved a sneak attack on a peaceful people who never saw it coming (me).

It was sort of like this:

Just like World War I, it lasted a lot longer and caused a LOT more problems than anybody expected, especially people who were totally innocent and didn't deserve it (me).

...and kind of like this:

And like all wars, when it was over, somebody had to write a book about it (me), so that historians of the future would know exactly what happened and whose fault it was (Reese's).

This is especially true of the part where the police got involved.

REESE

Calling it a war is kind of stupid. But Claudia always has to make a big deal out of everything.

I mean, yeah, it got out of hand for a while there. But it's not like anybody died.

Except on my MetaWorld account. THAT was a horrible, bloody massacre.

It wasn't actual blood or anything. It was pixels. But it was still pretty bad. There was, like, little red pixel blood splooshed all over the screen.

MetaWorld blood
(should be red, but Dad
won't buy color printer)

And that was all Claudia's fault, and totally NOT COOL. ⤷NOT my fault (see above)

I would never, EVER do something that mean to my sister. I'm nice to her almost all the time!

Except when she's mean to me first. And then it doesn't count.

Also, I had nothing to do with the cops. That was all Claudia. I have a totally clean record. Seriously! Call the cops if you don't believe me.

wait a few years—
this will change

MOM AND DAD (Text messages copied from Mom's phone)

Claudia says she's writing a book about the incident ← MOM

DAD → Like a novel?

No. Oral history. Interviews. Like that zombie book. But real

Great! If published, will look good on college apps

I'm worried it'll make us look like bad parents

How?

She wants us to participate

By interviewing us? I might have time after Entek deal closes. Getting crushed at work right now

No interview. Says she just wants to quote from our text messages

CHAPTER 1
THE GATHERING STORM

CLAUDIA

Here is some background information about The War:

My name is Claudia Tapper. I live in New York City, and I have two goals in life: I either want to be a famous singer-songwriter like Miranda Fleet, or the President of the United States.

Or both, if I have time.

My brother's name is Reese. He has no goals in life. Unless you count being a professional soccer player, which is totally unrealistic.

We are, unfortunately, twins. I am twelve years old. Reese is six.

I know what you're thinking. "Really? Is that possible?"

No. It's not. Reese is twelve, too.

He just has the brain of a six-year-old. A six-year-old that ate too much sugar and did not get its nap, so it has to run around our apartment and kick soccer balls against the wall and make noises like "GRONK!" and "SKADOOSH!"

Honestly, living with him is the most annoying thing ever. It's a pretty small apartment.

We live on the Upper West Side. But we go to school at Culvert Prep, which is across Central Park on the Upper EAST Side. My parents like to say the Upper West Side is more "down to earth." As far as I can tell, this basically means our neighborhood has more burger places, and not as many stores that sell $800 shoes. (Which, BTW, is insane. The shoes aren't even that cute.)

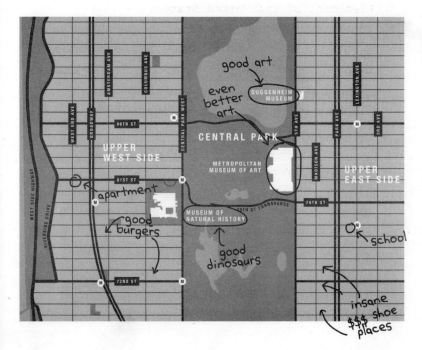

Culvert Prep is academically excellent, so there's no way Reese could have gotten in if he hadn't started going there in kindergarten. At that age, it's very hard for the admissions office to tell if a kid will turn out to be a total meathead.

Mom and Dad think Reese is perfectly smart, and he just needs to apply himself. They're wrong, but it's not worth arguing with them. If they had to admit the truth about their meathead son, it would make them incredibly sad.

And Dad is sad enough already, because he is a lawyer.

Anyway, back to Culvert Prep, which is where The War started.

Culvert Prep (mostly not meatheads) (except my brother) (and his friends)

To be totally specific, it started in the Culvert Prep cafeteria on Monday, September 8th, at approximately 8:27am. That's when Reese—in front of basically the whole sixth grade—launched a cruel and senseless sneak attack on me.

REESE

It didn't start at school. It started in our kitchen that morning, when Claudia ate my toaster pastry.

our kitchen (site of toaster pastry argument)

(me)   (Reese)

I paid $5 for these flowers at deli

CLAUDIA

That is SO not true. It wasn't even yours.

I only ate 2 of these

REESE

Yes, it was! There's six in a package. We each get three. And I only had two!

CLAUDIA

I only had two, too.

REESE

Liar!

CLAUDIA

It's true! I think Dad eats them when he gets home at night.

REESE

All I know is, brown sugar cinnamon's my favorite. And there was ONE left, and it was MINE.

And I was lying in bed, thinking, "Oh, man, I can't wait to narf that toaster pastry!"

Then I go into the kitchen, and you're, like, stuffing your face with it! And when I got mad, you laughed at me!

CLAUDIA

A) "Narf" is not even a word. And B) this is completely irrelevant.

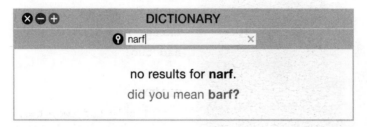

REESE

It's totally revelant!

CLAUDIA

Relevant.

REESE

Whatever! It's important! I NEVER would've made fun of you in the cafeteria if you hadn't eaten my toaster pastry! And then laughed at me about it!

The whole thing was your fault!

CLAUDIA

That is ridiculous. I'm not putting it in the book.

REESE

You HAVE to! It's the whole reason the war started!

CLAUDIA

No way. Not going in. It's MY book.

REESE

Then I quit. Do your own stupid interviews. I'm going to go play (MetaWorld.)

site of major battle
(like Gettysburg or
Waterloo)

CLAUDIA

Reese!
Augh! Fine. I'll put it at the end. Like a footnote or something.

REESE

No way. It goes in the actual book. Right at the beginning! This exact argument.

CLAUDIA

That'll ruin the whole thing! Have you ever SEEN an oral history?

REESE

I don't even know what one is.

CLAUDIA

It's like, different people telling a
story in their own words. But nobody, like,
stops to argue with each other in the middle
of it. ESPECIALLY not at the beginning.

REESE

This is supposed to be the true
story of what happened, right? And you're
recording it. So you have to put in EVERY
WORD I'm saying. Or your book is a big
skronking lie, and I quit.

⌐also not a real word

CLAUDIA

I hate you.

REESE

Duh.

CHAPTER 1½
THE STORM IS STILL GATHERING

CLAUDIA

I apologize for that last chapter.

But I had to leave it in because Reese talked to a lawyer. And the lawyer told him he could refuse to participate in the oral history if I didn't print our entire argument exactly how I recorded it on my iPad.

Which is ridiculous.

And I'm pretty sure the lawyer just told Reese that to make him shut up, because the lawyer was very tired from a long week of being a lawyer and just wanted to lie on the couch and fall asleep watching football.

lawyer (asleep on couch)

(lawyer's popcorn)

But when I went to complain, he was already snoring even though it was only the first quarter. And I didn't want to wake him up, because I am a kind and considerate person.

And I couldn't appeal to a higher court, because Mom was at yoga.

Just to be clear, though, this says Chapter 1½, but really it's Chapter 1, and you should just ignore that other Chapter 1.

Back to The War.

Historians disagree about where exactly it began. Some claim it started not at 8:27am in the Culvert Prep cafeteria, but an hour earlier, in the kitchen of Apartment 6D at 437 West End Avenue.

437 West End Avenue

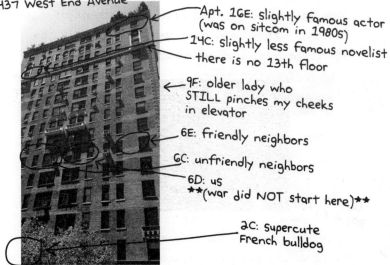

Apt. 16E: slightly famous actor (was on sitcom in 1980s)

14C: slightly less famous novelist

there is no 13th floor

9F: older lady who STILL pinches my cheeks in elevator

6E: friendly neighbors

6C: unfriendly neighbors

6D: us
(war did NOT start here)

2C: supercute French bulldog

These historians are idiots. And they can't even count to three.

Which, BTW, is the maximum number of toaster pastries I have EVER eaten out of a box of six.

But whatever.

Here's exactly what happened:

First of all, it's important to know that on a normal weekday at 8:27am, pretty much the whole sixth grade is hanging out in the cafeteria. So if you're going to launch a vicious sneak attack on an innocent person and want to make sure everybody hears it for the greatest possible humiliating damage, the cafeteria is the place to do it.

Second, it's even MORE important to know this: I was not the one who farted.

REESE

I still think it was you.

CLAUDIA

It wasn't! And we are NOT discussing this.

REESE

Because you had Thai food the night before, which totally makes you fart the next day.

I ate this...

Kai Kra Prow (Chicken with basil)............$8.95
Sliced chicken sauteed with onion, basil leaves, and chili pepper.

...BUT DID NOT DO THIS

And it smelled exactly like it did when we got off the bus that morning—

CLAUDIA

WE ARE NOT DISCUSSING THIS! NO, NO, ABSOLUTELY NOT—

REESE

—and I KNOW you farted on the bus, because I didn't just smell it, I HEARD—

CLAUDIA

INTERVIEW OVER! I'M TURNING OFF THE VOICE MEMO APP!

CHAPTER 1¾
THE STORM STOPS GATHERING AND STARTS STORMING

CLAUDIA

Sorry again.

I have decided not to even try to interview Reese about anything else until I can at least get to Chapter 2, because so far he is totally ruining my oral history.

Back to the cafeteria.

I was sitting with Sophie Koh, who is awesome and has been my one and only best friend since my original best friend, Meredith Timms, turned into a total Fembot and I had to take a vacation from not only being her best friend, but from even being her friend at all. Which is very sad and tragic, but is a whole other story.

Sophie and I were at the middle table by the window. I was telling her what happened in the latest episode of *Thrones of Death*, because Sophie's parents think she's too young to watch it. And they actually still have parental controls on their DVR.

Which is insane. But whatever.

THRONES of DEATH

MATURE AUDIENCES ONLY.
CONTENT WARNINGS

M L V T Q Z P B O G D

The Fembots were in their usual spot at
the next table over, talking about shoes,
or stabbing each other in the back, or
whatever it is they do. Sophie and I call
them "Fembots" because they all dress and
act exactly the same way and have no idea
how to think for themselves. And once when
we were telling Sophie's mom about them, her
dad overheard and said they sounded like
Fembots, which are supposedly these girl
robots from some movie I can never remember
the name of.

Anyway, "Fembots" is kind of perfect
for them. Athena Cohen is their leader, and
she is a total nightmare.

So the Fembots were on one side of us, and on the other side were Reese and his stupid soccer friends. Including Jens (actually pronounced "Yens") Kuypers, who is from the Netherlands and had just started going to Culvert the week before.

It's a little sad that Jens immediately started hanging out with Reese and the other soccer idiots. Because Jens does not seem like a soccer idiot at all. For one thing, he doesn't just wear FC Barcelona jerseys and warm-up pants all the time—he actually wears normal clothes, too.

For example, on the first day of school, he wore these really cool dark green pants with a button-down shirt and a brown vest that looked like it might be suede or something, and brown leather shoes that kind of matched the vest, but not quite. (Which was even better, because if they'd matched perfectly, it would have looked dorky.)

Also, Jens has high cheekbones and a very nice smile, which I know because he smiled at me on the first day when we were in line for trays at lunch and he let me go ahead of him. (This also shows that he has excellent manners, which is totally not true of any of the other soccer idiots.)

And because Jens is from the Netherlands—which means he is officially Dutch—he has this REALLY cool accent.

But even though Jens is not like the soccer idiots at all, I guess he started hanging out with them anyway because he is awesome at soccer. I wouldn't know, but that's what Reese says. And it makes sense, because Jens looks like he is very athletic.

So, Sophie and I were at the middle table in between the Fembots and the soccer idiots. There were also some other kids at the far end of our table, like Kalisha and Charlotte and Max, but they are not important to The War.

Except that one of them may have been the person who actually farted.

Culvert Prep cafeteria, Monday, Sept. 8th 8:27 AM

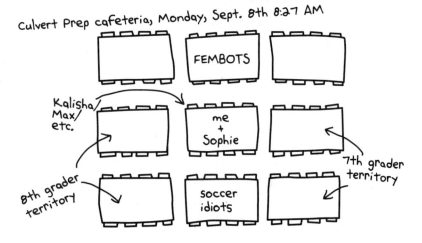

Sophie and I smelled the fart at almost exactly the same time. Her face scrunched up, and she put her hand to her nose, and I did the same thing, and we both went "Eeeew!" But not too loudly, because Sophie and I are mature enough to know that when somebody beefs, the polite thing is to not mention it and just try to avoid breathing for a while until it goes away.

Unfortunately, nobody else in the sixth grade is mature enough to know this.

And it was a very bad fart, so everybody smelled it.

Right away, Athena Cohen jumped up from her seat like a total drama queen and yelled, "Oh, that is DISGUSTING! Who DID that?"

The soccer idiots all started jumping up and making faces, and then Reese pointed at me and yelled, "IT WAS YOU!"

This was not only immature, but also totally unfair. Because, again, it was definitely NOT me.

So I said—in a very calm and mature voice considering the situation—"No, it wasn't."

But Reese wouldn't stop. He had one hand over his nose, and he was pointing at me with the other hand, and then he yelled, in a really loud and obnoxious voice, "JUST ADMIT IT, PRINCESS FARTS-A-LOT!"

And this is how totally immature the rest of the sixth grade is: everybody laughed.

The soccer idiots, the Fembots, even Charlotte and Max at the far end of the table.

It didn't matter at all that I was totally innocent, or that "Princess Farts-A-Lot" is not even funny. The whole world, or at least the whole sixth grade, was laughing at me for something I DIDN'T EVEN DO.

All because of Reese.

This, in case you couldn't tell, was the beginning of The War.

It was exactly like the sneak attack on Pearl Harbor that got America into World War II.

Well, not EXACTLY exactly, because there were no bombs, or ships, or planes, or actual death involved. But even so, it was horrible, and cruel, and totally unfair. And because I was so shocked and hurt, all I could do was say, "As if! Grow up, Reese!"

Or something like that. I can't remember exactly, because it was so stressful that my memory is kind of fuzzy. (I think this is what historians mean when they talk about "the fog of war.")

What I DO remember is that I had to grab my backpack and pretend to just casually walk away when really I was trying to get to the girls' bathroom ASAP so I wouldn't cry in front of everybody.

That is how cruel and horrible it was. It actually made me cry.

And because she is a true friend, Sophie went to the bathroom with me.

crying
took place
here

**SOPHIE KOH, best friend of
innocent victim**

You were really upset.
Because Jens was right there
when Reese said it, and—

CLAUDIA

Not because of Jens.
Because of everybody.
EVERYBODY laughed at me.

SOPHIE

Well, eventually you were worried about
everybody. But at first, you were all, "What
if Jens thinks I—" Why are you making that
hand gesture? What does that mean?

Ooooh!

Okay! Sorry.

*I have NO IDEA what Sophie
is talking about here*

So, um...yeah, it wasn't about Jens. At
all. It was...like...uh...

CLAUDIA

It was EVERYBODY.

SOPHIE

Totally. Like, I remember you were

crying, and—wait, can I say that? That you were crying?

CLAUDIA

　　Yes.

SOPHIE

　　Good. So, yeah. You were crying, and you were, like, worried it was going to stick, and everybody was going to call you "Princess Farts-A-Lot" for the rest of your life.

CLAUDIA

　　Which totally could have happened! Remember that thing with Hunter in fourth grade?   ↖ don't ask— it's disgusting

SOPHIE

　　Oh, yeah. People STILL call him "Booger Hunter" sometimes. So, yeah, I could see how you'd be worried about that.

CLAUDIA

　　And it DID happen! James Mantolini called me "Princess Farts-A-Lot" until practically Halloween.

SOPHIE

Yeah, but James is an idiot. Even the boys don't like him.

CLAUDIA

And remember Athena and Clarissa at lunch? When they shortened "Princess Farts-A-Lot" into just the initials—"P-FAL"—and then tried to get everybody to call me that?

SOPHIE

Ugh. They're the worst. But they only called you "P-FAL" for like a day.

CLAUDIA

It was longer than that. It was practically the whole week. And that first day was AWFUL. I literally thought it was going to scar me for life.

SOPHIE

I know. I'm so sorry! I remember in the bathroom you were really upset. Like, we were almost late to homeroom because it took you so long to stop crying.

CLAUDIA

You were SUCH a good friend. Like, I would still be in that bathroom crying if it weren't for you. Do you remember what you said to get me to stop?

SOPHIE

Yeah. I said, "Don't worry. We are going to take SERIOUS revenge on your stupid brother."

That really helped. Like, the second you started thinking about getting revenge on Reese, you stopped crying.

And then you started to get kind of psyched about it.

CHAPTER 2
PEACEFUL DIPLOMACY IS
A TOTAL FAIL

CLAUDIA

It is important to point out here
that even though I suffered a vicious and
emotionally devastating sneak attack, I did
not fight back right away.

The fact is, I am a completely peace-
loving person. Which means I did not go to
war until I had done everything I could to
solve the crisis through peaceful diplomacy.

REESE

You tried to get me in trouble is what
you did.

CLAUDIA

That is not true. Reese got HIMSELF in
trouble by attacking me. All I did was very
calmly explain the situation to Ashley when
she picked us up that afternoon.

Ashley is our after school sitter.
Although "sitter" isn't really the right
word for her job. Personally, I am mature

and responsible enough that I absolutely
DO NOT NEED babysitting. (Reese is a whole
other story, because he is a child and has
to be constantly watched so he doesn't burn
the apartment down or something.)

And Ashley is more like a substitute
parent than a sitter. She does all the
things Mom and Dad can't do because they're
at work—like cooking dinner, or yelling at
Reese to do his homework, or being there for
us when we need them.

At least, that's what she's supposed to
do. To be completely honest, Ashley is not
that great at her job. She spends 90% of her
time staring at her phone, and most of the
other 10% playing with her hair.

But she's VERY nice. And she lets me
watch *Thrones of Death*. So I'm fine with it.

It's kind of ridiculous that she's still
picking us up after school. But whatever.

**ASHLEY O'ROURKE, after school sitter/
substitute parent**

Wait, before we start—if this book
gets published, can you mention that I'm an
aspiring Broadway actress who's trained in
both Drama and Voice?

CLAUDIA

It's not really appropriate. But okay.

Ashley's head shot.
She soooort of looks like
this in real life.

To hire her as an
actress (or sitter), email
AshleyOnBroadway@gmail.com

ASHLEY

Thanks, Claude! You're the best.

Okay, so I'm trying to remember...I picked you guys up, I was totally on time—

CLAUDIA

For a change.

ASHLEY

Oh, stop. We got on the M79—no, it was before that. We were waiting for the bus. And you started telling me how, like, Reese had accused you of farting in front of everybody. And it was totally humiliating, and you were going to have to transfer to a new school out of embarrassment, and Reese needed to, like, get grounded for a year or something.

M79 bus: 15 min/day to & from school = 570 hours of my life spent on this (so far)

So I told Reese he had to apologize to you. And he said something like, "I'm sorry you can't take a joke."

And that just made it worse. You got crazy mad, and we got on the bus, and you guys like, wouldn't stop fighting. Like, all the

old people sitting up in front were turning
around to see what all the yelling was about.
   And that's when I emailed your mom.

ASHLEY (email to Mom)

From: AshleyOnBroadway@gmail.com
To: jpomeroy@scrimper.com
Date: 09/08/14 3:02:04 PM EDT
Subject: twins fighting

Hi J! Sorry 2 bug u but twins r in MAJOR FIGHT bc R
teased C in front of othr kids at school. C very upset.

I told R he needs 2 respect his sister.

I told C not 2 overreact like we talked abt over summer.

Both r not listening 2 me tho so can u talk 2 them when
u r home?

Also did u get turkey dogs b4 u left or should I buy more

Thx!
Ash

MOM AND DAD (text messages)

Ashley just emailed—Reese teased Claudia at school, very upset—can u come home early and give him "watch your sister's back" speech?

← MOM

DAD →

Have to finish brief tonight. Not home till at least 11. Can you do it?

I AM IN MOUNTAIN VIEW UNTIL FRIDAY

Oh. Right. Will come home and work from there

Try to get full story—if Reese's fault, take away MetaWorld for at least 24 hrs

How do I do that?

Seriously?

MetaWorld is computer thing, right?

OMG. That is just sad. It is all he talks about besides soccer

I know it's computer thing! Just don't know how to take it away. Do I hide his laptop?

Yes. Ask Ashley. Who is illiterate, BTW. Very scared that she is person supervising homework

At least she's not letting them watch Thrones of Death

CLAUDIA

Dad got home at 8:30 that night, which is really early for him. This made me think Reese was in big trouble.

And I'm pretty sure if Mom hadn't been on a business trip, Reese WOULD have been in big trouble, because she is much tougher than Dad when it comes to punishment. But Mom works for a very small Internet company that is trying to get a very big Internet company to buy them, so that whole week she was in California trying to get bought.

Mom's company logo. Not sure what they do. "E-commerce"?

I think history will record that
business trip as one of those totally
unfortunate things that, if it hadn't
happened, could have saved everybody a whole
lot of trouble. Like if that Archduke guy
(I forget his name, but it's on Wikipedia)
hadn't gotten shot before World War I.

Archduke just before getting shot.
That hat is CRAZY.

Because at this point, it wasn't even
really The War yet. It was still just The
Incredibly Cruel Thing Reese Did In The
Cafeteria.

And if Mom and Dad had punished
him enough—like if he'd lost ALL his
electronics for a week, not just his laptop
but his iPad, Xbox, TV privileges, and

even the totally ancient DSi that he only plays when Mom and Dad take everything else away—I would not have had to take the law into my own hands.

But after I very calmly explained to Dad what had happened, and he made Reese apologize—which only sounded halfway sincere because Dad was standing right there—he handed down Reese's sentence:

No laptop for a day.

Which was RIDICULOUS.

The only thing Reese uses his laptop for (besides homework, which he doesn't even do half the time) is MetaWorld. And when Mom and Dad take away the laptop, he just plays the mobile version on his iPad. Plus he'll claim he needs the laptop for homework, so they'll wind up giving it back to him for half the time he's supposed to lose it anyway.

I complained to Dad, but he wouldn't change his mind.

And I emailed Mom, but she said it was Dad's decision.

So diplomacy failed. It was obvious that the only way there was going to be any justice was if I went out and got some for myself.

And that meant revenge.

CHAPTER 3
OPERATION FISHY REVENGE

CLAUDIA

Here's what I was thinking when I came up with Operation Fishy Revenge:

Reese had accused me of stinking up the cafeteria in front of everybody, which was completely untrue. So I figured if I made him stink FOR REAL, everybody would get grossed out and laugh at him, and he would realize how terrible it felt.

So it'd not only be totally appropriate, but also an important learning experience.

And the best way I could think of to make Reese stink was to hide a dead fish in his backpack.

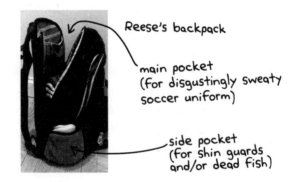

Reese's backpack

main pocket
(for disgustingly sweaty soccer uniform)

side pocket
(for shin guards
and/or dead fish)

He takes the backpack practically everywhere with him, so it's almost as good as hiding a dead fish in his pants. And much less complicated.

The big question was where to get the fish. I wanted to go to Chinatown, because they have tons of fish for sale down there, and most of them are already dead. Plus their prices are very low. And you can get really exotic kinds, like octopus. (not technically a fish)

But it was Monday night, and I have guitar on Tuesdays and Student Government on Wednesdays. So the earliest I could get to Chinatown was Thursday, and that was only if I could convince Ashley to take me there, because my parents won't let me ride the subway alone.

This, by the way, is completely stupid, since A) the subway is actually very safe, because half of the scary-looking people sitting on the platforms are actually undercover cops in disguise; and B) I know how to hold my house keys in my fist with the points sticking out so I can gouge the eyes out of anybody who messes with me. But whatever.

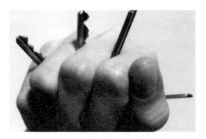

house keys =
excellent deadly weapon
(esp. on subway)

And I wanted revenge sooner than Thursday. You know how people say, "Revenge is a dish best served cold"? They are totally wrong. If you ask me, it's much better to get your revenge when it is still warm from the heat of your anger. Plus you don't have to carry the anger around all bottled up inside you for too long, which is very unhealthy. So I decided to get a fish from Zabar's because it's right at Broadway and 80th Street and has tons of seafood.

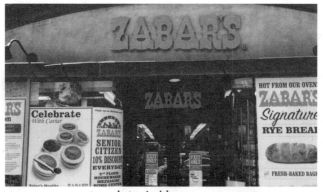

Zabar's. Try the chocolate babka—
it is delicious

Sophie was going to help me pick it
out, but she couldn't make it on Tuesday.

SOPHIE

Tuesday's bad for me. I have ballet AND
violin.

CLAUDIA

Sophie is way overscheduled.

Anyway, I brought $20 of my birthday
money to school that day, and after
Ashley picked me up from my guitar
lesson, I told her I wanted to get a
snack, but that it was totally fine for
me to go to Zabar's by myself, and I'd
meet her at home.

Ashley was fine with that. This is
the kind of thing that makes me question
her judgment, but since it lets me get
away with stuff like buying a dead fish
to put in my brother's backpack, I'm not
complaining.

I ended up getting a porgy, because
they look totally freaky and were only $5.99
a pound. The one I got was a pound and a
half and cost $8.94 total.

porgy: looks bad, smells worse

On the way home, I sniffed the bag a couple of times, and it already smelled horrible. Which was perfect.

Getting the fish into Reese's backpack was easy. When he comes home from soccer, he throws it in the coat closet by the front door. So I waited until he was taking a shower and Ashley was busy making dinner. Then I went to the coat closet.

I got out the pack, unzipped the little side pocket where Reese keeps his shin guards (which, BTW, smelled worse than the fish), and opened up the Zabar's bag.

The fish was wrapped in paper inside a Ziploc, so getting it out without sliming myself was a challenge. Plus, my heart was beating really fast, and at one point Ashley banged a pot in the kitchen, which scared me so much I almost dropped the fish. But I managed to slide it in behind the shin guards, zip the pocket shut, and toss the pack in the closet.

Then I went into the building hallway and put the Zabar's bag in the trash compactor chute to dispose of the evidence.

trash compactor chute (evidence disposed of here)

Mission accomplished!

All I had to do was wait until the next day, when the fish would start to stink in the middle of school and Reese would wind up humiliated.

I never once considered the possibility that my brother could be so clueless that he'd carry a rotting fish in his backpack for a whole week without noticing it.

But he was.

REESE

The thing is, I don't use that pocket for anything but shin guards. And we didn't scrimmage at practice on Thursday, so there was no reason to open it until Saturday.

It's not like I was thinking, "Oh, man, I better check all my pockets just in case somebody smooged a dead fish in there."

Anyway, the smell wasn't too bad the first couple of days.

not an actual word

CLAUDIA

That is crazy. It stank right from the beginning. By the next morning, it had stunk up the whole closet so much I was worried I'd ruined all our coats. I could even smell it when everybody was hanging out in the cafeteria before school. But since nobody else seemed to notice, and I wanted people to figure it out for themselves and blame Reese, I kept my mouth shut.

When I got home from Student Government

that afternoon, Reese had already put his backpack away in the coat closet. The stink was so awful in there that I actually moved my coats into my bedroom closet. I felt bad about leaving everybody else's coats in there, but if I'd moved them, it would have looked totally suspicious.

That was Wednesday.

On Thursday morning, I avoided the closet completely, because I was too scared to see what it smelled like. But I could smell the fish the whole way to school on the bus, and also in the cafeteria that morning.

It seriously reeked.

Nobody else seemed to notice it, though. Which was starting to get very annoying.

REESE

I definitely started smelling something fishy at one point. But I just thought it was like when you go to the seashore and it's stinky everywhere. I figured, New York's close to the seashore. That's why it stinks.

actually surprised Reese knows this

Other people smelled it, too. Like, I remember Mrs. Berner sniffing the air in

English class on Thursday and going, "Okay, who stepped off a fishing boat?"

And that same day, Kalisha Hendricks, who sits behind me in math, poked me and said, "Is that you? That nasty smell?"

I sniffed my armpit, and I said, "Does it smell like a man?"

And she said, "Yeah, Aquaman."

Then she sniffed the air and went, "DEAD Aquaman."

That was pretty funny. Kalisha's hilarious. Plus, she's awesome at math. I actually wish she sat in FRONT of me, because then I could copy off her without turning around.

Anyway, the fish was definitely getting kind of reeky by Thursday. In the locker room after soccer, everybody got in a big fight over whose shoes were making the whole place stink.

But that was pretty funny, too.

CLAUDIA

By Thursday night, it seemed like Operation Fishy Revenge was backfiring. I could NOT believe how clueless my brother was.

And I was getting very worried about the rest of the coats in the hall closet.

So right before dinner, I secretly went and got Reese's backpack—which was so rank I would have bailed on the whole thing and gotten rid of the fish, except that by then I was too grossed out to even unzip the pocket—and moved the backpack out of the apartment to our building's emergency stairwell.

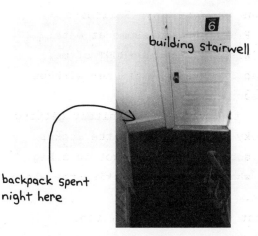

building stairwell

backpack spent night here

Friday morning, when I got up extra early to move it back to the closet again, the whole stairwell smelled like a fish store in Chinatown.

After Reese and I had left for school, Dad must have opened the coat closet for the first time since Tuesday.

MOM AND DAD (text messages)

DAD →

I think a mouse died in coat closet. REALLY stinks in there

Did you get rid of it???!!!

← MOM

No time. Had to go to work. Left message for Ashley to search closet

Did you take coats out???

Didn't think of that

ERIC!!! Calling Ashley now

CLAUDIA

Friday morning in the cafeteria, I was sure Reese was going to get what was coming to him. But even though everybody could smell the stink by now, nobody nailed Reese for it.

People did seem to figure out it was

coming from the general direction of the
soccer idiots. At one point, Athena Cohen
lectured them about their bad hygiene. But
that was as close as anybody came to blaming
Reese.

I tried to nudge people along. At one
point, I said, "Reese, I think YOU might be
what stinks."

But then his stupid friend Wyatt went,
"Whoever smelt it, dealt it, Princess Farts-
A-Lot!"

So I had to back off.

SOPHIE

It was CRAZY smelly by Friday morning.
We were cracking up about how nobody could
figure out where it was coming from.

Actually, you weren't cracking up. You
were kind of mad about it.

CLAUDIA

I was, like, half-mad, half-worried.
Because I didn't know how it was going to end.

REESE

At one point in math class, Ms.
Santiago brought in two other teachers to

try and figure out what the smell was, and they were all wandering around the room sniffing things.

The same thing happened in English. But James Mantolini is in both of those classes with me, and I just figured it was him. He's the kind of person you'd totally believe would smell like dead fish on purpose.

CLAUDIA

By the time I got home Friday afternoon, Ashley had emptied out the coat closet, and all the coats were in a couple of huge piles on the couch.

They all smelled like dead fish. Ashley had the windows open, but I was starting to freak out that this was going to end with me getting in a ton of trouble.

Fortunately, though, Reese had an early soccer game the next morning in Brooklyn. Since Wyatt's mom was driving them to the game, Reese stayed overnight at the Templemans', and he took his backpack with him.

REESE

Mrs. Templeman is kind of uptight, and

she keeps their house super clean. So she
started complaining about the smell pretty
much the minute I walked in the door.

Wyatt Templeman's
actual house (crazy
huge for NYC—his dad
owns hedge fund)

    I left my backpack up in Wyatt's room.
Then we went down to the kitchen to get a
snack, but all they had was fruit and some kind
of organic popcorn that tasted like cardboard.

    We were eating the cardboard when I
heard Wyatt's mom scream.

    Then there was this "Ka-blam-ka-blam-ka-
blam!" on the stairs, and a second later Mrs.
Templeman ran through the kitchen yelling
"AAAAAH!" and holding my backpack in front
of her.

She went straight out the door into their back yard. Almost nobody in New York City has a yard, so you'd think it'd be totally cool that Wyatt does. But the Templemans' back yard is mostly just plants and furniture, and whenever we try to play soccer out there, Mrs. Templeman yells at us.

So it's actually not that cool.

Templeman back yard (for NYC, this is ENORMOUS)

Anyway, we followed Mrs. Templeman out there to see what the screaming was about. My backpack was sitting on the patio, and she was backing away from it with her hand on her mouth like she might barf.

Then she said, "Reese—what is that THING in your backpack?"

And I was like, "What thing?"

And she pointed at it and went, "THAT THING."

So I went over and looked in the side pocket, and that's when I saw the fish.

It was pretty nasty.

At first I was, like, "Eeew."

Then I was, like, "Huh. That explains the weird smell."

And then I was, like, "How did that fish get in my backpack?"

I thought maybe it could've jumped in. Except I hadn't been that close to a river in a while.

Then Mrs. Templeman got a garbage bag.

Actually, no. First, she called Mom.

MOM AND DAD (text messages)

Ellen T just called—smell in closet likely from dead fish in Reese's backpack

What???

Call me

Calling you now

CHAPTER 4
THE FISHY AFTERMATH

CLAUDIA

One of the problems with any war is that sometimes innocent civilians get hurt. In this case, the innocent civilian was Reese's backpack.

And I guess Mrs. Templeman, too.

But I feel especially bad about the backpack.

Also, the shin guards.

REESE

If it was up to me, I wouldn't have thrown away the shin guards. It's not like they didn't work anymore. They'd just been sitting next to a dead fish for a couple of days.

But Mrs. Templeman wouldn't even let me take them out of my backpack. Instead, she made me empty everything else out of it and put all my stuff in the wash. Then she made me put the backpack in a garbage bag and knot it up. Then she made me and Wyatt throw the bag away in a can on the corner so it wouldn't stink up the house.

Final resting
place of Reese's
backpack

I tried to argue with her, but she
said my mom had agreed on the phone that we
should throw out the backpack.

On the way to the corner, Wyatt and I
opened up the bag to get another look at the
fish. It was pretty gross. Wyatt dared me to
touch it, and I was going to pick it up and
throw it at him just to be funny. But then
Mrs. Templeman yelled at us from her stoop,
and we had to cut it out.

After that, she dragged us to Modell's
and bought me new shin guards. I felt bad,
because I could tell she was pretty annoyed
at the whole thing.

Even though I'd lost my backpack and my

shin guards, I wasn't that angry at first. Mostly, I was just confused about where the fish came from. The next day at the game—we beat FC Riverdale 4-1, and I had a beastly assist—I asked the rest of the team about it. Nobody knew anything. But Xander said I must have made the Mafia mad, because they send dead fish to people whenever they're going to kill them.

Xander is EVIL— more on him later

That got me worried. I don't know anybody in the Mafia, but I think James Mantolini is Italian, and he can be pretty nuts. So I asked Dad about it after the game. He said there was no way James Mantolini was planning to kill me, and it was just somebody playing a prank.

He also told me it's not cool to think somebody's in the Mafia just because they're Italian.

On the way home, he took me shopping for a new bag. That's when I REALLY got mad— because it turned out they no longer sell my exact bag, and the new version only has one side pocket. So now I have to keep my water bottle in the main pocket, and it splooshes around in there and gets my homework all wet.

After that, I knew I had to find out

not an actual word

who put the fish in there. Because I didn't
realize how awesome my bag was until it
was gone.

And it was up to me to avenge its death.

CLAUDIA

I once left my favorite purse on the
M79 bus, so I know what it's like to lose
something that's as important to you as
Reese's backpack was to him.

I really do feel bad about that. If I
had it to do over again, I would've put much
more thought into what would happen to the
backpack after I put the dead fish in it.

I also would've put much more thought
into what I was going to say if anybody
asked me about the situation. Because
being honest and trustworthy is EXTREMELY
important to me. People who lie about
things—like my former best friend, Meredith
Timms—are the absolute worst.

I am NOT one of those people. I do not
tell lies. Ever.

Except this time.

When he came home from work Friday
night, Dad asked me if I knew how a dead
fish had gotten into Reese's backpack. Until

then, I didn't even know the dead fish had been found, so I was totally unprepared for the question.

It didn't help that Dad had just walked in while Ashley and I were watching *Violent Housewives*. I'm supposedly not allowed to watch it, and I was holding the remote, so I had to switch to the Disney Channel super fast. I was still kind of flustered from that when Dad asked about the fish.

totally stupid but very entertaining show

Basically, I panicked. Instead of telling Dad the truth, or saying something like, "A dead fish in his backpack? That is the STRANGEST THING I ever heard"—which sounds like a denial but technically isn't, so I could always go back later and prove that I hadn't really lied to him—I just flat-out denied the whole thing.

I think my exact words were something like, "Eeeew! A dead fish? No way! I wouldn't even TOUCH a dead fish! That's disgusting!"

In the short term, this was fine. Dad didn't ask any follow-up questions, and after Ashley left, we ordered in Chinese food and had a pretty fun night until Dad

<< 58 >>

slightly less stupid show
(but also less entertaining :( )

fell asleep on the couch watching *Super Future Star!* with me.

But Mom got back from her business trip on the redeye Saturday morning, and that night all four of us went out for sushi. Even before the edamame showed up, Mom said to Reese, "So how did this dead fish get into your backpack?"

Reese said he figured it was just somebody playing a joke.

And Mom said, "I don't know. Seems like a lot of trouble just for a joke. Mrs. Templeman said it was a pretty big fish."

Then Reese told Mom his theory about James Mantolini and the Mafia, which was ridiculous. I saw James's dad at a school play once, and the only way he could be in the Mafia is if he's their accountant.

James Mantolini's dad
(I googled this)

(he should prob change his
Facebook privacy settings)

Mom thought it was ridiculous, too. She also thought it was ethnically insensitive, so Reese got a whole lecture about how you shouldn't stereotype people, and the Mafia's not even that powerful anymore, and almost every country has some kind of organized crime, so it's not just the Italians, and besides which, Italy has a rich history and culture that goes back thousands of years, blah, blah, blah.

Then she said something like, "Is there anybody at school who's mad at you?"

And Reese said, "No. Everybody likes me."

Then I snorted.

I didn't mean to. It just sort of came out involuntarily.

The second I snorted, Mom snapped her head around and gave me this *look*, and I knew I was about to get busted.

I had to cover fast. "That's ridiculous!" I told Reese. "I can name AT LEAST five people who don't like you."

"Like who?" said Reese.

This was tough, because for reasons I will never understand, people actually do like Reese.

"James Mantolini," I said. "Sophie,

sometimes..." Then I got stuck. And to make things worse, Mom was drilling a hole in my head with her eyes.

"Claudia," she said in her mad-but-trying-not-to-yell-because-we're-in-a-restaurant voice. "Did you put the fish in his backpack?"

REESE

Right away when Mom said it, I knew it was you. It was SO OBVIOUS!

CLAUDIA

This is when things got a little sketchy for me, morality-wise.

THE TEN COMMANDMENTS

false witness = lying
(see? sketchy)

"...or thy parents"

Because I had like a tenth of a second to decide whether to admit the truth—not just about the fish, but about lying to Dad—or dig in.

I dug in. Which in this case meant acting like I was totally offended, and I couldn't believe they'd accuse me of something like that, and even crying a little bit. I also told Mom she'd know what a ridiculous accusation it was if she was around more often and not away on business trips all the time. (This was very unfair, but also very effective, because Mom feels tons of guilt about spending too much time at work.)

Basically, I made kind of a scene.

The whole time, Reese was freaking out because he was convinced it was me.

And the elderly couple at the next table were getting really annoyed at us.

And I think we scared the waiter a little.

I am not proud of any of this. If I had it to do over again, I would tell the truth.

But it worked.

In fact, it worked so well that Mom and Dad wound up getting mad at Reese for refusing to believe I was innocent.

REESE

NOT a typo. My brother actually talks like this.

It was CRAY! She was totally lying, and they believed it! And then they started yelling at me for getting mad at her!

I was so skronking angry I could barely eat my California rolls. — also not a typo (or an actual word)

CLAUDIA

So I got away with it.

Except I didn't, really. Because I felt awful for the whole rest of the weekend. Lying like that makes you feel totally gross. And for days afterwards, I walked around scared that Mom and Dad would somehow find out the truth, and I'd be in five times as much trouble because I was guilty of both the fish thing AND lying about it.

You know that story about how George Washington chopped down a cherry tree, and when he got busted, he admitted it right away, because he couldn't tell a lie? I totally believe that happened. But I don't think George Washington told the truth because he was noble. I think he did it because he was very, very smart, and he knew lying is almost always WAY more trouble than it's worth.

Honestly, it would have been MUCH less painful if I'd just confessed. I probably would've had to use the rest of my birthday money paying for the new backpack, and Mom and Dad might've taken away all my electronics for a week or something.

But it would have been worth it not to feel all guilty and worried.

The guilt was so bad that by the time I went to bed on Sunday night, I'd decided that not only was I done trying to get revenge on Reese for the "Princess Farts-A-Lot" episode, but I was going to spend the rest of my life being really, really nice to my brother.

REESE

When I went to bed that night, I dreamed about payback.

Because IT WAS ON.

CHAPTER 5
REESE STRIKES BACK
(SORT OF) (BUT NOT REALLY)

CLAUDIA

Even though this is my book, I am basically giving Reese this entire chapter. Mostly because I still feel bad about his backpack.

REESE

It was totally cray for Claudia to ruin my backpack and get away with it! But by the time we left the sushi place, I knew I was on my own. The authorities were helpless.

I was like Batman in that one movie— like, he's the good guy, but everybody THINKS he's the bad guy, even though the truth is he's the only one who can stop the real bad guy.

Who was my sister.

I had to think about it for a while, but eventually I came up with the perfect revenge: putting a dead animal in Claudia's backpack.

Not a fish, though, because that'd be
copying. *dead animal = also copying*
(Reese = not creative)

Except there was one problem: fish are
the only dead animals you can buy. You can
buy PARTS of other ones, like a chicken leg
or something. But it's super hard to find a
whole dead animal for sale.

And I felt like it had to be the whole
animal for my plan to really work.

For a while, I thought maybe I could
find one just lying around, like a pigeon or
a rat. But I spent some time looking around
on the street, and I couldn't find any.

I was actually glad about that. It's
not like I wanted to pick up a dead pigeon.

But if I couldn't buy one or find
one, I was pretty much out of luck, dead-
animal-wise.

Unless I wanted to kill something *True. R can't*
myself, and I'm not so into that. ← *even kill*
water bugs
in the tub.

So I decided to get Xander involved,
because he's good at thinking up stuff
that's kind of gross and also a little mean.

CLAUDIA

I'm sorry—I know I promised to give

this whole chapter to my brother, but there are two things everyone needs to know about Xander Billington.

First, he is the devil. Seriously. He might even be worse than Athena Cohen, which is saying a lot.

Second, Xander likes to tell people he's "old school." And he totally is, but not the way he wants to be. He's not the cool kind of old school—he's the OLD kind of old school.

Here is what I mean by that: back in first grade, when Mrs. Beres was telling us the story of the first Thanksgiving and the Pilgrims who came to America on the *Mayflower*, Xander yelled, "My great-great-great-great-great-great-grandfather was one of them!"

Everybody thought he was lying, including Mrs. Beres. But it turned out to be true. ⟵―――――― Xander lied a lot in 1st grade (also 2nd–6th grade)

Xander is ACTUALLY RELATED to somebody who was on the *Mayflower*.

Which is why it's so completely ridiculous that he tries to talk like a rapper from the South Bronx.

THE LANDING OF THE PILGRIMS AT PLYMOUTH, MASS. DEC. 22ᵈ 1620.

XANDER BILLINGTON, soccer idiot/*Mayflower* descendant

Reese was all, "Yo! Top secret project!" And I was down with that.

But then he was all, "I want to creep something stanky into my sister's backpack."

And I was all, "Yo, that is WAY too easy. Duh! Poop."

REESE

I couldn't do poop. It was just too nasty. I mean, whose poop would I use? Mine? Eeeeech.

And using somebody else's poop would be ten times worse.

XANDER

I was all, "Fine, what-eva. Get some stinky cheese, yo."

REESE

THAT was a good idea. Except it had to be weird cheese. Normal stuff like cheddar doesn't even really smell that bad.

I went to Zabar's, because they have a whole counter full of weird cheese. I picked up some of the wedges and started sniffing them, and the guy behind the counter went, "Can I help you?"

Zabar's cheese counter: stinky but delicious

And I went, "What's your smelliest cheese?"

And he went, "Apwas."

[Editor's note: I do not know how to spell this cheese name.]

[Editor's note #2: If you hadn't guessed, the editor is me, Claudia.]

But the Apwas was $27.99 for a little round box. Which was cray! I mean, I wanted revenge and all, but not $27.99 worth of it.

So I went, "What's your SECOND-smelliest cheese?"

And he went, "Gorgonzola."

The great thing about the Gorgonzola was you could get just a tiny wedge of it. Which still cost $3.82. But I had five bucks, so I was okay with that. I was going to tell Ashley the cheese was for a science project, but she didn't even ask why I bought it.

Ashley can be kind of spacey.

Claudia must have been expecting me to try to mess with her, because when I got home, her backpack wasn't lying around anywhere—she had it in her bedroom, and the door was closed.

So I had to play it cool for a little while.

CLAUDIA

I'm sorry. I hate to keep interrupting Reese's chapter. And I don't want to be mean to my mentally challenged brother. But what he's saying is completely ridiculous.

First of all, I wasn't expecting Reese to mess with me at all. The reason my backpack wasn't lying around is because I am a responsible person who puts her things away where they belong. My backpack is NEVER just "lying around."

Second, Reese did NOT play it cool. At all.

He came charging into my room, looking all excited and holding a Zabar's bag. When he saw me sitting there, he got all deer-in-the-headlights confused for a second.

Then he yelled "WAZZZZZUUUP!" and ran right back out again.

At that point, I had a little mental argument with myself.

On the one hand, I suspected the Zabar's bag was something gross and smelly he was planning to hide in my room, or possibly my backpack. On the other hand, even though Reese is not exactly the most brilliant mind of his generation, I didn't think he'd be so incredibly lame and uncreative that he'd try to get back at me by doing EXACTLY what I did to him.

So I decided to give him a little test.

I poked my head into his room and said, "I'm going to go for a walk. Do you want anything from the store?"

Which, if he had even the tiniest little speck of a brain, he would have realized was very, very suspicious.

Then I left the house for ten minutes.

REESE

Eventually, Claudia went out for a while, and I snuck into her room and hid the cheese in one of those little outside pockets of her backpack next to a pack of gum and some hair scrunchies.

my backpack

homework

gum/
hair scrunchies

Gorgonzola found here

I actually hid it TOO well, because
even though it started to stink right away,
it took her two days to find it.

CLAUDIA

It took me two MINUTES to find it. Not
even. It was more like two seconds.

What took me two days was deciding how
to respond.

The first thing I did was get an airtight
storage container from the kitchen, seal the
stinky cheese in it, and stick it way back
in the rear of the fridge.

The second thing I did was call Sophie.
When I explained the situation to her, she
had a brilliant idea.

SOPHIE

I was like, "Why don't we eat it?"

CLAUDIA

Brilliant. Seriously.

But it was Tuesday when I called her,
so Sophie was on her way from ballet to
violin. And we're both busy Wednesdays,
which meant the cheese had to stay in the
fridge until Thursday.

REESE

By the second day, the cheese in Claudia's backpack stank like crazy. I could smell it from halfway across the cafeteria.

CLAUDIA

Reese is out of his mind. The cheese was in the fridge THE WHOLE TIME.

But I've never told him that, so the only way he'll ever find out is if he reads this book. Which, now that I think of it, is actually an excellent way for me to tell if he ever reads it. He says he will, but I doubt it. The only book Reese has ever read that wasn't assigned in school was a Pokémon handbook when he was eight years old. And even then he mostly just looked at the pictures.

I'm getting off track here. Back to the cheese.

REESE

It stank so bad that Xander went up to my sister in the cafeteria and yelled, "YO, CLAUDIA—WUT UP WITH YOU STANKIN' LIKE ROTTEN CHEESE?"

And then Claudia said, "I don't know—maybe it's 'cause I've been standing next to your mother?"

I have to admit that was pretty funny. Everybody laughed except Xander. He got really mad.

Like, kind of a little TOO mad. Xander's got a temper.

CLAUDIA

Xander is also the world's biggest idiot. The cheese was literally a mile away when he said that.

But the thing is, I shouldn't have humiliated him in front of everybody like that. Because it turned him into my sworn enemy.

And like I said before, Xander is evil. Which made him a MUCH more dangerous enemy than my brother.

Like, if this was World War II, Reese was basically Italy—definitely a bad guy *[Editor's note: Weird that Italy was a bad guy in World War II, right? I was very surprised to learn this, too. But it's right there on Wikipedia.]*, although not the bad guy people were really worried about, because Italy is just not that scary.

And Xander was Germany—a WAY more serious bad guy whose leader I'm not going to mention here, because Dad says you should never, ever compare anybody to that particular person, since he was so much more evil than anyone else in history that if you bring him up in an argument, you will just look ridiculous.

But his name rhymes with "Fitler."

And in this War, Xander was definitely Rhymes-With-Fitler.

But more on that in the next chapter.

Thursday afternoon, Reese was at soccer, so Sophie came over after her Korean class, and we ate the cheese on some crackers. All I can say is, Gorgonzola is delicious. Although I don't get why it's called Gorgonzola when it's really just blue cheese. ← "bleu?"

While we ate it, we talked about whether I should get back at Reese for trying to stink up my backpack or just forget the whole thing. On the one hand, I still felt bad about ruining his favorite backpack. And the way he'd tried to get back at me was not just a total fail, but also very sad and pathetic.

On the other hand, I didn't want him to think he could mess with me and get away with it. I felt like that would send a message of weakness.

SOPHIE

What was that thing you quoted? From the guy who was president before we were born?

CLAUDIA

"This aggression will not stand."

SOPHIE

You are so smart! Where did you learn that?

CLAUDIA

I saw it in a movie about bowling.

Anyway, even though I definitely believed his aggression should not stand, I didn't want to do anything TOO mean. At this point, The War still wasn't even really a full-on war. It was more like an exchange of

hostilities. And I wasn't going to be the
one to escalate it into anything crazy.

That's why I finally decided the best
thing was to just mess with Reese's head a
little.

REESE

Claudia must have found the cheese
while I was at soccer practice. Because when
I came home that night, she was waiting in
my room for me.

CLAUDIA

You know that thing evil geniuses do in
old movies where they're sitting with their
back to you, and then they spin around
slowly in their chair and tell you their
evil plan with a wicked smile on their
face?

That's what I did. I even had a little
stuffed animal in my lap that I was petting
like it was a cat. Because for some reason,
evil geniuses usually have pet cats.

Reese didn't get what I was doing at
all, though, because he never gets jokes if
they're even a little bit clever.

evil genius   evil cat

REESE

She was sitting at my desk chair,
and when I came in, she went, "Hellooooo,
Reese," in this weird voice like she had a
bad cold.

And I went, "What are you doing in my
room?"

And she went, "I hid your cheese.
HAHAHAHA!"

CLAUDIA

Ugh! He's totally messing up my lines.
I did this whole evil-genius speech in a
fake British accent. It went like this:

"Hello, Reese...I've come to thank

you for the delicious gift of your cheese.
Sadly, I'm lactose intolerant. So I've
chosen to return it to you. And since you're
so obviously fond of playing hide-and-
seek, I've placed it in a secret location
somewhere in your room. Best of luck finding
it before the fumes overpower your senses,
slowly driving you to the brink of insanity.
MWAH-HAH-HA-HA-HA!"

I'm not actually lactose intolerant.
That was part of the joke.

And it was hilarious. Seriously. Or it
would have been, if I hadn't wasted it on
somebody who wasn't smart enough to get it.

Even so, the look on my brother's face
when I told him I'd hidden the cheese in his
room was pretty great.

REESE

I spent, like, an hour looking for the
cheese before I gave up. Claudia hid it
REALLY well. But I figured eventually it'd
start to stink bad enough that I could track
it down just by the smell. And sure enough,
after a couple of weeks, my closet started
to reek so bad I knew the cheese must be in
there somewhere.

But I still can't find it. And Claudia won't tell me where it is.

So I'm stuck with a closet full of reeky cheese that I can't find. It's pretty gross.

CLAUDIA

I have no idea what's making Reese's closet stink like that.

But it is DEFINITELY NOT CHEESE.

(Eeeeeew.)

CHAPTER 6
FITLER JOINS THE WAR

CLAUDIA

Up until now, The War had been pretty one-sided. Ever since Reese's cruel and unfair sneak attack on me in the cafeteria, I had basically kicked his butt all over the map. So I figured he'd learned his lesson, and that'd be the end of it. Even if he hadn't, he wasn't clever enough to launch a counterattack that could really hurt me.

Unfortunately, The Cheese Incident (which, if this were French class, I would call *L'Affaire du Fromage*) had a major and completely accidental side effect: it brought Xander into The War as an enemy combatant.

And Xander is the devil. Or at least the devil's incredibly obnoxious, thinks-he's-cool-but-is-actually-an-idiot little punk nephew.

REESE

I was mad angry at Claudia by now. She ruined my backpack AND my closet! AND she got away with it!

Both times!

If I didn't do something, I was going
to spend the rest of my life getting pwned
with dead fish and smelly cheese.

*not a typo
(google it)*

Plus, it was making me feel like a
loser. There's this team in our soccer
league, Knickerbocker FC, that gets beat
like 9-0 every game. They're a total
doormat, and everybody either laughs at
them or feels sorry for them. That's how it
was getting to be with me. I was like the
Knickerbocker FC of my own family.

I didn't like that at all. I needed a
win, bad.

But the good news was I had somebody
else on my team now. Because after Claudia
ripped on him in front of everybody with
that joke about his mom, Xander was almost
as mad at my sister as I was.

And when Xander gets mad, he gets even.

XANDER

I was all, "Yo! We gots to PWN her,
babylicious! We gots to HAMMER DOWN on that!"

CLAUDIA

Honestly, it is the saddest thing ever
that Xander talks like this. I almost feel

sorry for him that he thinks it's cool. (I bet Fitler was a total fail at being cool when he was in junior high, too. Come to think of it, that would actually explain a lot about world history.)

REESE

Xander said if we really wanted to mess with Claudia, the thing to do was to get other girls involved. Because according to Xander, girls are like sharks—when they smell blood, they all go nuts and swarm in for the kill.

Fembots at the beach

XANDER

True dat. Most of the time, boys just be playing. Like, a boy'll smack you down, and then be, like, "It's all good, Bro-seph." And then you're cool again.

But girls don't play, yo. They are
VICIOUS. They will cut you deep.

And they all be on ClickChat 24/7,
rilin' each other up.

REESE

When Xander told me all we had to do
was post something nasty about Claudia
online and all the girls in our ClickChat
circle would blow it up huge, that kind of
made me nervous.

Because even though I hate Claudia,
she's still my sister.

But Xander promised it wouldn't be
THAT bad. Like, it'd be bad for a couple
of days. And then everybody'd forget
about it.

So I was like, "Okay. What do we post?"

And he was like, "What's the straight-
up nastiest thing she does?"

I thought about it for a while, and all
I could think of was sometimes when she's
watching TV in the living room and she
doesn't think anybody's looking at her, she
picks her nose.

And Xander was like, "YO! That is stone
cold! But we need video."

So we decided he should stay overnight at my place. That way, we could stake out the living room with our iPads until we caught Claudia picking her nose on camera.

MOM AND DAD (text messages)

Reese wants to have Xander overnight Saturday

← MOM

DAD → Do we like Xander? I forget

We do not. He is kid who broke end table at birthday

Oh, THAT Xander

Yes. And we owe the Templemans so I'd rather have Wyatt over instead

You can't do that

Can't do what?

Swap kids

Sure I can

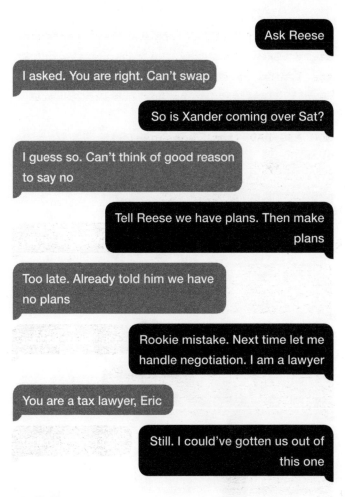

Ask Reese

I asked. You are right. Can't swap

So is Xander coming over Sat?

I guess so. Can't think of good reason to say no

Tell Reese we have plans. Then make plans

Too late. Already told him we have no plans

Rookie mistake. Next time let me handle negotiation. I am a lawyer

You are a tax lawyer, Eric

Still. I could've gotten us out of this one

CLAUDIA

First of all, let me just say that when I am a parent someday, I will not be a total pushover who lets my kid hang out with a complete psychopath just because he wants to.

Second, I am going to be completely honest here: everyone on earth picks their nose. That's just a fact.

But people with good manners never, ever do it in public, or when company is over. Especially when that company is an evil little worm.

So Reese and Xander's plan was doomed to failure.

Unfortunately for me, they wound up getting video of something just as bad.

Actually, it was worse.

REESE

All I can say is, if I knew how bad things were gonna get, I NEVER would've posted that video on ClickChat.

CLAUDIA

Whatever.

Here's what happened: after dinner on Saturday night, I started watching an episode of *Super Future Star!* in the living room. But Reese and Xander kept poking their heads in

from the hallway, giggling like idiots and
holding up an iPad like they were recording me.

Even though I wasn't sure why they were
doing it, it was annoying enough that I
bailed on the TV and went to my bedroom.

Then I hung out with Sophie and Carmen
and Parvati on ClickChat for a while until
they started talking about *Coven of Angels*,
which is this incredibly stupid book series
about teenagers who live in San Francisco in
some future world where witches control the
government, and all the cute boys are dead
and come back as ghosts or something.

world's stupidest
book series

There are, like, ten of these books,
and they're not only ridiculous but very

badly written, and I can't understand why
anybody on earth likes them, let alone my
friends. But instead of arguing with them
for the hundredth time about how stupid
Coven of Angels is, I signed off and decided
to play some guitar. ← world's greatest guitar

I got out my Stratocaster and started
messing around. Pretty soon, I came up with
a really cool riff, and a song started to
form in my head.

This happens a lot, which is a big
reason why one of my two goals in life is
to become a famous singer-songwriter like
Miranda Fleet. I know people think that's a
long shot career-wise. But when you think
about how many shows like *Super Future Star!*
are out there, and how many totally lame
singer-songwriters have had hits lately, it
seems doable to me. So whenever I come up
with even a rough idea for a song, I record
it in GarageBand so I don't lose it in case
it turns out to be a hit.

Of course, not all of my rough ideas
turn out to be great. Or even good.

And even great songs can start out
pretty rough.

Which is why when I record something, it's

meant to be FOR ME AND ONLY ME until I have
time to rework it and really make it awesome.

The problem is that when I put my
headphones on to record, I get totally
wrapped up in what I'm doing. And I forget
all about things like the fact that my
brother is having a sleepover with an evil
little worm and they are both desperate to
take me down hard.

Which is how "The Vest Song" wound up
on ClickChat and ~~basically~~ ruined my life.
totally

REESE

After Claudia went in her room, Xander
and I figured the nose-picking video wasn't
going to happen. So we decided to wait until
she fell asleep, then sneak into her room
and put one of her hands in warm water and
one of them in cold water. Xander said this
was guaranteed to make her wet the bed, and
if we got it on video, it'd be even more
embarrassing than picking her nose.

We started playing MetaWorld in my
bedroom to kill time. After a while, Xander
went to the bathroom, and when he came
back, he said, "Yo, does your sister have
a cat?"

I said, "No. Why?"

He said, "'Cause some animal be gettin'
strangled in her bedroom."

XANDER

Straight up, yo: That girl CAN. NOT.
SING.

CLAUDIA

That is ridiculous. Like Xander knows
the first thing about singing.

REESE

We went out into the hallway and stood
next to Claudia's door. And sure enough, she
was singing in this weird squeaky voice—

CLAUDIA

It's called a falsetto. I'd been trying
out a bunch of different vocal styles, and
this just happened to be a falsetto.

Because, like I said, the song was just
a ROUGH IDEA that I was playing around with
and HAD NO INTENTION OF ANYONE EVER HEARING
EXCEPT ME. I was EXPERIMENTING.

Which, BTW, is something ALL artists do.

REESE

Well, I don't think the experiment worked.

CLAUDIA

Duh! THAT'S WHY THEY'RE CALLED "EXPERIMENTS."

REESE

And it wasn't just the squeaky voice. The guitar was all weird and, like, thrummy—

CLAUDIA

Because it wasn't amplified! ALL electric guitars sound weird and thrummy if they're not amplified!

REESE

Whatever. So we decided to get it on video. And the locks on the bedroom doors in our house are totally easy to pick—you just stick a scissor blade in them and turn it sideways.

CLAUDIA

I am totally making Mom and Dad buy me a dead bolt for Christmas.

I seriously need one of these.

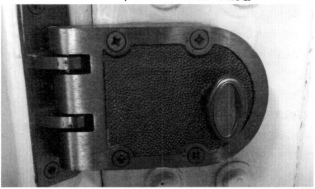

REESE

So we got a pair of scissors, opened the door, and ba-ZING! Two minutes later, we're uploading this video to ClickChat of Claudia singing a love song to Jens—

CLAUDIA

IT WASN'T ABOUT JENS!

REESE

Um, hello? "That cute leather vest, it's really the best, with an accent so smooth, like a musical groove"?

CLAUDIA

They were TEMPORARY LYRICS! And that could've been anybody!

REESE

Oh, sure. 'Cause you know, like, a THOUSAND people with leather vests and foreign accents—

CLAUDIA

GET OUT OF MY ROOM!!!!

REESE

But we're not done with the oral history—

CLAUDIA

OOOOOOOUUUT! I HATE YOU!!!!

CHAPTER 7
THE CLICKCHAT ATROCITY

CLAUDIA

I apologize for losing my temper at the end of that last chapter. I could have edited it out, but I think it's important to leave it in as proof that the scars of war run deep, and that people who are involved in such conflicts often have emotional problems that last for years after the fighting has stopped.

I am going to try to get through this next section very quickly, because even now, just thinking about it makes me want to cry.

And also stick hot needles under my brother's fingernails.

First of all, it is very, very important to understand that the song I was singing was A) definitely NOT about anyone in particular; B) actually about a lot of different things, not just vests and foreign accents; C) not even called "The Vest Song," which is a name Reese and Xander totally made up; D) a very rough first take that

I fully intended to rewrite and rerecord, definitely without a falsetto (because I agree it wasn't working); and E) absolutely, positively NOT MEANT TO BE HEARD BY ANYBODY BUT ME.

For the rest of my life, when I record anything, I am going to sit facing the door so I know if someone's poking their head in with an iPad to secretly record me.

I am also never, ever going offline again for more than fifteen minutes. Because if I'd been on ClickChat that night and caught it early, it wouldn't have been so bad. But I'd turned off my phone and the Wi-Fi on my laptop so I wouldn't get interrupted while I was recording. And when I finished playing guitar, it was late enough that I went right to bed without bothering to go back online.

So I had no idea what had happened until the next morning, when I turned on my phone and found twenty-seven new text messages.

Sixteen were from Sophie. The rest were from Carmen and Parvati. For the historical record, here are a few of Sophie's texts:

SOPHIE (text messages)

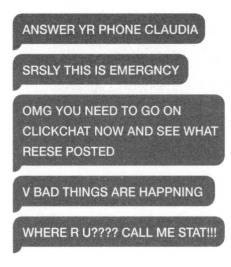

ANSWER YR PHONE CLAUDIA

SRSLY THIS IS EMERGNCY

OMG YOU NEED TO GO ON CLICKCHAT NOW AND SEE WHAT REESE POSTED

V BAD THINGS ARE HAPPNING

WHERE R U???? CALL ME STAT!!!

CLAUDIA

After seeing Sophie's texts, I was pretty much in full panic mode before I even opened ClickChat. And what I found on Reese's feed was so horrible that when I first saw it, I got a stabbing pain in my chest like I was dying of a heart attack.

For the record, here is what it looked like (minus the actual video, which eventually got deleted). I only included the first 15 comments—by the time Reese deleted the video, there were 135 of them:

skronkmonster

sorry!
DUH_VEST_SONG.mov
has been removed by user

❤ 214 likes

goddessgurrl OMG!

mdith_timms ikr?

goddessgurrl guys shes singing about Jens

lingurding EPIC FAIL

lurvlyc hahahahahahaha!!!!!!!!!

i_m_ batman_4realz my dog heard this and now he's howling

tasha_sez Miranda Fleet call ur agint u r in TROUBLE hahaha

goddessgurrl so sad. there is no way Jens likes her

sophie_k_nyc Reese this is NOT FUNNY Claudia will hate u

mdith_timms what is Jens username? someone should fwd

lurvlyc MY EARS...THEY BLEED...

sophie_k_nyc srsly Reese DELETE THIS NOW

goddessgurrl shut up Sophie. cant you take a joke?

mdith_timms yea we r just appreciating her awesome talent <3 <3

lingurding omg Claudia shld probly move to Alaska or sumthing

<< 99 >>

CLAUDIA

Trust me when I say the next 120 comments were even worse. Which is why, as soon as I made sure I wasn't actually dying of a heart attack, I went to Reese's room to kill him.

REESE

Xander was right—after we posted the video, the girls in our grade (plus a few boys, but mostly it was the girls) all went totally nuts in the comments section. It was actually kind of scary how nuts they went. Like, even before we went to bed, I'd started thinking it might have been a bad idea to post the video.

CLAUDIA

"MIGHT HAVE BEEN"???

REESE

I'm sorry! Anyway, we were up pretty late, so I was still asleep when Claudia came in and started kicking Xander.

CLAUDIA

I was NOT kicking him. I am a peaceful person.

He just happened to be lying in a sleeping

bag on the floor, and it's a very small room. So on my way over to your bed, I accidentally hit him with my foot about five or six times.

REESE

If you weren't kicking him, why was he screaming?

CLAUDIA

Because he is weak. I AM A PEACEFUL PERSON.

REESE

If you're so peaceful, why'd you start punching me?

CLAUDIA

You're my brother. It's different. Besides, you totally deserved it.

REESE

It's not fair! You know I can't hit you back.

CLAUDIA

Because you're weak, too.

REESE

No! 'Cause you're a girl!

CLAUDIA

That is totally sexist, Reese.

REESE

Fine! Next time, I'll hit you.

CLAUDIA

Like to see you try.

REESE

Will you just chill? I've apologized, like, fifty times for this!

CLAUDIA

It's never enough.

REESE

Can we get back to the moral history?

CLAUDIA

Oral history.

REESE

Whatever. So, all the yelling woke up Dad. And he came in and separated us, and that's when you got all hysterical and totally freaked him out.

But he had to deal with it, because Mom
was at the gym.

MOM AND DAD (text messages)

> TOTAL TWIN MELTDOWN PLEASE
> COME HOME ASAP

Is anyone hurt????

> Not physically. But Claudia hit Reese

Can't you deal? Only good spin class
all day starts in 5 min and I have not
worked out in ages

> This is way over my head. Lots of
> tears and girl stuff

Eric, YOU MUST DEAL. I will be back
by 11:00

> OK but no promises kids will be in
> one piece when you return

MAN UP!!! You wanted kids

REESE

I deleted the post even before Dad told me to. Because I seriously did feel bad about it. Like, even when I was lying in bed the night before, I was thinking, "Maybe I should delete it."

CLAUDIA

BUT YOU DIDN'T.

REESE

Well, Xander was there, and...I'm sorry! Really! I am. It's, like, the stupidest thing I've ever done. Are you ever going to forgive me?

CLAUDIA

Hmm. Let me think.
NO.

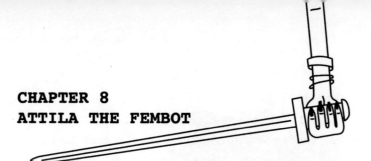

CHAPTER 8
ATTILA THE FEMBOT

CLAUDIA

By the time Mom got back from her spin class, Dad had sent Xander home, taken away all of Reese's electronics, and grounded him indefinitely.

And this is how horrible what Reese and Xander did to me was, and how ugly the comments on ClickChat got: Reese did not even try to argue about his punishment.

Not only that, but after Mom heard the whole story and watched the video on Reese's laptop—right before she made him delete the file forever—she didn't try to make me feel better by saying things like, "Oh, honey, it's not so bad" or, "Sweetheart, I know it's annoying, but try not to blow it out of proportion."

Instead, she took me shopping for shoes and let me get a pair of boots that were way too hot and weren't even on sale.

way too hot/not on sale

But before we went shopping, she called Xander's mom and had a long conversation with her in the bedroom with the door closed.

XANDER

Yo, that was WEAK, getting moms all up in my bizness. But it was a fail, yo. 'Cause I was clean. Ain't nothin' on MY

ClickChat wall but skate videos. All
that "fan page" ish? That was some otha
bruthas.

Actually, it was sistas.

CLAUDIA

If the "Vest Song" nightmare had ended
when Reese took the video down, it would
have been bad enough.

But it was about to get even worse.

Because at some point between Saturday
night and Sunday, the Fembots created
a "Fans of Claudia Tapper" wall on
ClickChat.

As far as The War went, the Fembots
getting involved was like...I don't even
know. It was MUCH crazier than anything in
normal world history.

It was like if right in the middle
of World War II, when America was totally
focused on trying to beat the Nazis,
Attila the Hun suddenly came out of
a time machine and ransacked half the
country.

Seriously.

Attila the Fembot

I didn't find out about "Fans of Claudia Tapper" until that Monday morning. I'd been dreading going to school that day, because basically the whole sixth grade had seen "The Vest Song," and I knew just walking through the halls was going to be a nightmare.

But even though their ClickChat comments were the absolute worst, the Fembots weren't even my biggest worry. The person I was REALLY worried about seeing was Jens Kuypers.

Because even though the song was absolutely NOT about him, everybody thought it was. So I figured he must think I was some kind of insane stalker or something.

And of course, practically the first person I saw that morning was Jens.

Although it actually wasn't THAT bad.
Because he is such an incredibly kind and
thoughtful person, Jens made a point of
smiling and saying "Hi, Claudia!" in this
really cheerful voice. Which was very cool
of him, except that I knew he was only
doing it to be nice, so it kind of just
made me more embarrassed. I couldn't even
look him in the eye, and afterwards I
decided it'd be better to completely avoid
him for a while.

Like a year. Or maybe two.

I was still recovering from seeing
Jens when I walked past the Fembots. They
were all clustered around Athena's locker,
and when Clarissa Parker saw me, she went—
in this REALLY snotty voice—"Ohmygosh,
Claudia, have you SEEN your fan page?"
Then they all laughed like it was the most
hilarious thing ever.

I got a sick feeling in my stomach,
because I knew they were up to something evil.

I ran to the lounge (which is the only
place you can use a phone during school
hours) and logged on to ClickChat.

When I saw the fan page, I got even
more sick to my stomach.

CLICKCHAT POSTS ON "FANS OF CLAUDIA TAPPER" WALL

ClaudiasBiggestFan This is a page dedicated to the greatest singer in the history of the universe. Post all your favorite videos of Claudia's AMAZING singing here!

ILoveClaudia She is the best EVAH! This is my favorite!

ClaudiaSuperstar Whenever she sings I get tears in my eyes <3<3<3

CLAUDIA

In case you can't tell from the screenshots, those were videos of A) a howling dog, B) a toddler throwing a temper tantrum, and C) a Mongolian throat singer (I don't even know what "throat singing" is, but it is NOT good).

The rest of the comments on the page were so awful I couldn't even look at them long enough to take screenshots.

Even though "Fans of Claudia Tapper" was all done with fake names, it was obvious who was behind it. Because Athena is the most sarcastic person on the planet. And since she became a Fembot, Meredith is, like, the second-most sarcastic person on the planet. The whole page was basically Sarcasm Central. With a side order of Vicious and Cruel.

It was the worst day ever. By lunchtime, my sick feeling had turned into stabbing pains. I called Mom from the school nurse's office, and she didn't even try to convince me to stay in school. She let me take a cab home, and she asked Ashley to come in early and bring me my favorite kind of soup.

That's how bad it was. But don't take my word for it:

SOPHIE

Honestly, that fan page was, like, the meanest thing I've ever seen in my life. It was even worse than some of the stuff on *Violent Housewives*.

PARVATI GUPTA, friend

The Fembots are just so vile. If karma exists, Athena and Meredith are going to come back to life as cockroaches.

Fembots reincarnated

Not even, like, normal cockroaches. Deformed ones. That all the other cockroaches will make fun of. And Clarissa and Ling will be, like, bacteria or something.

CARMEN GUTIERREZ, friend/political ally

It was just so wrong! Somebody had to do something to stop them. Cyberbullying is a VERY serious issue. Like, even before you mentioned it, I was thinking about bringing it up in SG.

CLAUDIA

"SG" is Student Government. I am sixth grade class president, and Carmen is not only my second-best friend but also my closest ally among the class representatives. And she decided—almost without my having to suggest it—that it was time for the SG to lobby Culvert Prep's administration to outlaw cyberbullying.

Tied with Parvati. So, best friend ranking is
1) Sophie
2) Carmen (tie)
2) Parvati (tie)

Which was SO great of her. Carmen is awesome. Plus, she takes her class rep job VERY seriously.

And it was much better that she brought up the cyberbullying issue instead of me. Because pretty much the whole school was talking about "The Vest Song" and the Fembots' stupid fan page. So if I'd brought it up, it'd look like I was trying to get them in trouble.

And I am not the kind of person who'd do that. I would NOT use my political power to go after my enemies, even if they deserve it.

Although I did help Carmen prepare thirty-two pages of research on cyberbullying that she presented at Wednesday's SG meeting.

CARMEN

At first, Mr. McDonald *[Editor's note: Mr. McDonald is the SG's faculty advisor.]* seemed like he wasn't really on board. He was all, "You know...if it's not happening on school property...can we really legislate it?"

But then he saw that article you gave me about the high school that got sued in Arizona and had to pay some kid a million bucks.

School Pays $1M in Cyberbully Case

And that pretty much scared him into changing his mind.

CLAUDIA

At Wednesday's meeting, by a vote of

17 to 4, the Student Government officially passed a resolution proposing a policy of zero tolerance for cyberbullying.

"Zero tolerance" basically means that if you bully another student online, you'll automatically get suspended from school, with no exceptions.

But for any Student Government resolution to become official policy, it has to get approved by the Vice Principal in charge of student discipline. And Mrs. Bevan was kind of lukewarm on it.

JOANNA BEVAN, Vice Principal, Culvert Prep Middle School

I completely agree that Culvert needed a policy to address cyberbullying. It's the twenty-first century—this issue isn't going away.

But I did have some reservations about zero tolerance. As an administrator, I'm always wary of "one size fits all" punishments.

CLAUDIA

Fortunately, when I showed Mrs. Bevan

the story about the school in Arizona that got sued for a million dollars, she decided her reservations weren't that big a deal. She announced the new zero tolerance policy in a school-wide email on Thursday.

The email went out at 4:17pm. By 8:36pm, the "Fans of Claudia Tapper" wall had permanently disappeared from ClickChat.

Coincidence?

I don't think so.

So basically, Attila the Fembot got back in her time machine and quit ransacking my life. At least for the time being.

Which was good, because I needed to get back to focusing on The War. As vile as the Fembots were, they never would have created that stupid page if Reese and Xander hadn't uploaded "The Vest Song" in the first place.

So Reese and Xander had to be dealt with.

By this point, Reese was doing his best to be nice to me. But it was too little, too late. **WAAAAAAY too little**

REESE

I felt really bad about the whole "Vest Song" thing. And when I read that stuff Mrs. Bevan wrote in the email about how we should all have a code of conduct for how we act online, I decided to come up with a code of my own.

Not just online, though. For everything. I decided I was going to be a Person Who Chooses To Be Kind To Others At All Times, No Matter What.

And I really meant it! I wasn't going to tease people, or say mean things, or do anything mean at all to anybody, ever.

ESPECIALLY Claudia.

I was going to be the nicest brother in history.

CLAUDIA

Too little. Too late.

CHAPTER 9
OPERATION STUPID HAIRCUT

CLAUDIA

After The ClickChat Atrocity, I decided to dedicate my life to making Reese and Xander suffer a public humiliation at least a hundred times worse than the one they'd put me through.

This turned out to be kind of hard.

For one thing, Operation Fishy Revenge had taught me my brother was very difficult to humiliate. Things that would make a normal human being so embarrassed that they'd consider moving to a whole other state—like, say, smelling like a dead fish for three days—didn't really seem to faze him.

And Xander's barely human, so I figured he'd be even harder to embarrass.

Not only that, but it had to be a stealth humiliation. I didn't want Reese and Xander—ESPECIALLY Xander—to get any ideas about attacking me again. So whatever I did, I had to keep my fingerprints off it.

In the end, it took me a whole week to come up with a plan.

It would have taken even longer if
Rodrigo Barrando hadn't gotten a Mohawk.

Dad says I can't use actual photo of Barrando unless I pay huge $$$ for legal rights

REESE

Rodrigo Barrando is the world's awesomest
soccer player. Seriously. He's a beast. If you
don't believe me, search "Rodrigo Barrando best
goals" on YouTube. That one against Liverpool
in the Champions League last year was NUTS.

He also has awesome hair.

CLAUDIA

I will admit that Barrando used to have
pretty great hair. He was actually cute
until he went and got that Mohawk, which was
a seriously bad idea, because his head is
totally the wrong shape for it.

I mean, nobody looks good in a Mohawk.
But Barrando REALLY doesn't look good in one.

REESE

I thought it looked beast! He did it
for, like, charity or something.

Claudia came in when I was watching him get interviewed on *The Header*, and she was all, "Ohmygosh, he looks like a COMPLETE PSYCHOPATH."

And I was all, "He looks AWESOME!"

CLAUDIA

That's what got me thinking that if I could convince Reese and Xander to get Mohawks, they'd show up at school thinking they looked awesome, and everyone would laugh at them.

And then they'd realize they looked ridiculous. But it'd be too late, because there's nothing you can do to get rid of a Mohawk except to shave your head, which would look EVEN MORE ridiculous.

So they'd be stuck looking like idiots for WEEKS.

It was genius.

All I had to do was figure out how to trick them into getting Mohawks.

REESE

I remember at breakfast one morning, Claudia was like, "You should get a Mohawk."

That seemed kind of random.

CLAUDIA

I knew it wasn't going to be that easy.
I was just testing the waters. And Reese's
answer was actually very helpful. He snorted
and went, "Yeah—like Mom would ever let me."

Which made me realize the real challenge
wasn't going to be convincing Reese to get a
Mohawk—it was getting the idea past my mom.
Not to mention Xander's parents, who I figured
weren't going to be too psyched about it, either.

So I needed to create a situation where
they'd get Mohawks without asking their
parents first.

And I didn't know how things worked over
at the Billingtons', but in our apartment,
haircut appointments are Ashley's job.

along with groceries/dentist/soccer ball replacement (Reese)/etc.

ASHLEY O'ROURKE, after school sitter

All I can say is, under normal
circumstances, there is no way I would
ever let your brother get a Mohawk without
checking with your mom first. Like, NO WAY.

CLAUDIA

This was why I had to create some kind
of Mohawk crisis situation.

<< 121 >>

Not to be mean, but Ashley isn't
good in a crisis. I know this from
experience. First, she panics. Then she
looks around for somebody to tell her what
to do.

And she's willing to take orders from a
twelve-year-old if it means she doesn't have
to make a decision by herself. So in the
right crisis, I was pretty sure I could get
her to approve the Mohawk.

But creating a situation in which your
brother ABSOLUTELY HAS TO GET A MOHAWK IN
THE NEXT HALF HOUR, so there's no time for
Ashley to get in touch with Mom to sign off
on it, is not easy.

It's not like you can get good ideas
for this kind of thing online. If you google
"Mohawk crisis situation," there's just
not a lot out there except for some actual
crisis involving the real Mohawk tribe,
which is totally unhelpful when all you want
is a bad haircut.

So it took me a while to come up with
the Barrando Charity Video idea.

Once I did, though, creating the fake
email account was easy.

FAKE EMAIL (sent to Reese Tapper and Xander Billington)

✕ ← ⇐ → ✉

From: BarrandoFanClub@gmail.com
To: BarrandoFanClub@gmail.com
BCC: SKRONKMONSTER@gmail.com, XlzKillinIt@gmail.com
Date: 10/08/14 3:02:04 PM EDT
Subject: SPECIAL OFFER FOR NYC FANS OF
BARRANDO!! HURRY!!

Ola! New York City Fans of Barrando!

We have for you a special offer ONLY FOR YOU!

As you know, Rodrigo is in your city TODAY ONLY
OCTOBER 8TH filming his special charity video to help the
children with special diseases!

Any Barrando fan 12 years old or smaller WITH A
MOHAWK HAIRCUT JUST LIKE BARRANDO can show
up to the special video shoot IN THE CENTRAL PARK
"SHEEP MEADOW" AT 4:45 PM TODAY and be a star in
the video with Barrando himself!

If you do not have MOHAWK HAIRCUT, we are sorry but you CAN NOT BE IN THE VIDEO OR MEET BARRANDO.

You must have MOHAWK HAIRCUT to participate and meet your idol!

See you TODAY OCTOBER 8TH AT 4:45 PM in the Sheep Meadow with your Mohawk!

Arriba!

Hector Dominguez

El Presidente, Barrando Fan Club
New York City Chapter

CLAUDIA

I thought I did a pretty good job with the fake email considering that I don't know any Spanish. In fact, I was so proud of it that I showed it to Sophie and Carmen.

They actually got a little offended.

CARMEN GUTIERREZ

I just think it's kind of uncool to make fun of non-native English speakers. Recent immigrants face a LOT of challenges that, tbh, I think you might be a little blind to as a member of the dominant culture.

CLAUDIA

I know. And I'm totally sensitive to that! I swear I wasn't trying to make fun of non-native English speakers. I was just imitating one to fool Reese and Xander.

SOPHIE KOH

I dunno. That's kind of a gray area.

CLAUDIA

But I can't explain the Mohawk situation without the email. How about I include it, but also put in an apology to anyone who might get offended?

CARMEN

Good idea.

SOPHIE

Yeah. That's smart.

CLAUDIA

For the record, I would like to officially

apologize to anyone who might have thought my email was offensive and/or not cool.

I would also like to point out that I only sent it to Reese and Xander. Who are idiots. And can barely read anyway.

The timing of the email was critical, because I had to send it when A) Reese and Xander would be checking their email and B) there would be JUST ENOUGH time for them both to get Mohawks and make it to the spot where the video was supposedly shooting, but C) NOT enough time for Ashley to get in touch with my mom.

So I waited until the next Wednesday afternoon, when Reese and Xander didn't have soccer and my mom was on a plane to California, so she couldn't get text messages.

I had Student Government after school that day, but right before it started, I sent the email. Then I waited five minutes, excused myself from the meeting, and called Reese.

REESE

I was on the bus with Ashley when Claudia called me. She was all, "Did you

hear about this Barrando video thing?
EVERYBODY'S talking about it."

And I was all, "Huh?"

And she was like, "Check your email!
Hurry!" Then she hung up.

I thought that was kind of weird. But
I checked my email, and I found this thing
from, like, the "Barrando Fan Club"—which I
didn't even remember signing up for—but it
was like, "Get a Mohawk and come to Central
Park and you'll meet Barrando!"

And I basically went nuts and started
begging Ashley to take me to the haircut
place over on Columbus.

ASHLEY O'ROURKE (texts to Mom)

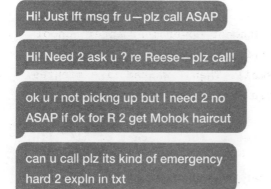

Hi! Just lft msg fr u—plz call ASAP

Hi! Need 2 ask u ? re Reese—plz call!

ok u r not pickng up but I need 2 no
ASAP if ok for R 2 get Mohok haircut

can u call plz its kind of emergency
hard 2 expln in txt

CLAUDIA

I figured Ashley might need a little push, so I waited a few more minutes, then stepped out of Student Government again (when Mr. McDonald asked why I kept leaving, I told him I was having lady problems, which always freaks out male teachers and gets them to stop asking questions) and called Ashley.

ASHLEY

So, Reese had gotten this weird email about some soccer player who was going to make him a movie star if he got a Mohawk in, like, ten minutes.

I couldn't get your mom on the phone to approve it, and your brother was, like, totally freaking out. And then you called me, and you were like, "Hey, Ash, I just wanted to say I heard about this Mohawk thing from the kids at school, and I think Reese should totally go for it, because YOLO! And also if he misses out he'll totally regret it for the rest of his life, and—"

Wait. Why are you asking me about this?

CLAUDIA

No reason.

ASHLEY

I thought this interview was just about the big fight between you and—OHMYGOSH! CLAUDE! Was the Mohawk thing part of it?! Like, did YOU send that email?

CLAUDIA

Umm...maybe.

ASHLEY

CLAUDE!!! How could you DO that??? You got me in serious trouble!

CLAUDIA

Sorry, Ash!
[Editor's note: Oops! I totally forgot that until now, nobody knew I was behind the Mohawk email.]

ASHLEY

That was seriously not cool, Claude. Like, your mom was RIPPED when she called me that night.

MOM AND DAD (text messages)

DID YOU SEE THIS???

OMG. That's not real, is it?

IT'S REAL. THAT IS YOUR SON'S HEAD

Did you tell him he could do that?

I DID NOT. VERY VERY ANGRY AT ASHLEY

Could be worse

SHE PAID $75 FOR THAT MOHAWK

Calling you now

ASHLEY

Not only that, but Reese and I had to wander around Central Park looking for some nonexistent video shoot for, like, two hours. He was practically crying when he couldn't find it.

REESE

It was the weirdest thing. Like, not only was there no video shoot, but when I googled "Barrando news" online, I found out he wasn't even in America that day. *[Editor's note: Reese still has no clue that I sent the email.]* And the next day, the only other person who said he even got the email was Xander. Which is cray! 'Cause he hates Barrando.

XANDER

Barrando sucks, yo. Everybody on Barcelona sucks. REAL MADRID FO-EVA!

CLAUDIA

I did not realize Xander hated Barrando.

Which, obviously, meant the Xander front of Operation Stupid Haircut was doomed from the beginning. And even though it worked brilliantly as far as tricking Reese into getting a Mohawk, it still turned out to be a total fail because of one thing I never anticipated.

REESE

I'm still bummed I didn't meet Barrando or get to star in a video with him, but I'm really glad I got that email.

If I hadn't, I never would've gotten a Mohawk. Which was BEAST!

CLAUDIA

He loved his Mohawk.

Like, seriously loved it. He could not have been more thrilled with his ridiculous-looking haircut.

Even worse, all his soccer idiot friends loved it, too.

REESE

It totally freaked out kids on other teams. Like, the next game, I stole three balls in a row from some kid on City Kickers, and I'm pretty sure it's all because he was scared of my hair.

I just wish Mom would let me get another Mohawk.

MOM AND DAD (text messages)

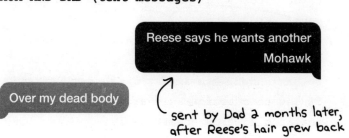

sent by Dad 2 months later, after Reese's hair grew back

CHAPTER 10
THE WAR COMES TO
PLANET AMIGO

CLAUDIA

Operation Stupid Haircut was a real setback. But when it was over, I realized if I wanted to win The War, I had to start thinking like my enemies.

I mean, public humiliation was the worst possible punishment I could think of for ME. And also for anybody with a brain. But Reese and Xander could care less about it, because they were too immature to feel shame. You know how little babies walk around naked, just letting their business hang out all over the place, because they don't know any better?

Mentally speaking, that's pretty much where Reese and Xander were at. Which meant if I wanted to make them feel pain, I had to hit them in a place where they actually felt it.

So I asked myself: what does Reese REALLY care about? What's the most important thing in his life?

And how can I destroy it?

There was only one answer.

Actually, there were two. But one of them was his soccer team, and destroying Manhattan United would hurt too many innocent bystanders. Like Jens Kuypers, who plays "striker" (whatever that is) and is such an incredibly kind person that he actually friended me on ClickChat a couple of days after the whole "Vest Song" horror show. Which, just like when he said hi to me in the hallway, was very sweet of him but only made me feel even more lame, because I knew it was just a pity-friending.

So if I couldn't go after the soccer team, that just left the one other Most Important Thing In Reese's Life:

MetaWorld. Which I was totally clueless about.

Because as far as I was concerned, only idiots played MetaWorld.

So I had to do some research. I got a MetaWorld account, and here is the first thing I realized, which was a real shock:

MetaWorld is actually really, really cool.

MetaWorld

MetaWorld is a sandbox indie video game in which players create three-dimensional environments on planets they design themselves. Beginning with MetaWorld 2.0, players can play in "Society" mode, in which they create economic and political structures for their planets...

It isn't so much a video game as a whole bunch of video games mashed into one. Depending on what mode you're in, there are a TON of different ways to play MetaWorld.

For example, the first night I got my account, I used Society mode to create my own planet. I called it "Claudarama," and I made everybody who lived there artists and musicians, because that's the kind of planet I'd want to live on.

But since everybody was busy making art, nobody was growing any food. So there was nothing to eat. And right away, all my artists started starving to death.

So I had to create a bunch of farmers.
Plus factory workers, and teachers, and
all kinds of other people, because it
turns out if your society is full of just
artists and musicians, it will pretty much
collapse.

So that was very educational.

Then I decided to create a castle
for Claudarama's ruler, President
Claudaroo. But to raise enough money
to build an awesome one, I had to crank
up my planetary tax rate to 70%. *would've looked like Taj Mahal (if I'd finished it)*

Which must have been way too
high, because before I even started
building the castle, everybody went
on strike. Including the artists and
musicians.

Which was a real slap in the face,
seeing as how I'd created them.

To get everybody back to work, I had
to build a pretty serious police force and
knock some heads. I felt bad about that,
but if you don't want your planet to be
a hot mess, you have to make some tough
choices.

Again, VERY educational.

MetaWorld "Society" Mode

After I got the strike problem straightened out, I was going to go back to building my castle. But then I looked at the clock and realized it was almost midnight and I hadn't started studying for my French test the next day.

Like I said, MetaWorld is really cool. It's actually a little TOO cool, because it's totally addictive.

And at first, I was confused, because it was the kind of cool that Reese would never, ever be into. It was way too interesting and smart for him.

Then I discovered Conquest mode.

MetaWorld

...MetaWorld 3.0 introduced a new gameplay mode, "Conquest," in which players can do battle in both multiplayer arena combat and unlimited, at-large warfare...

THAT made a lot more sense. There was no way Reese was spending hundreds of hours online just building stuff and making sure his planet's economy didn't fall apart.

But killing people? Totally his thing.

At first, I assumed he was killing people on a planet of his own, and if I wanted to take him down, I'd have to turn Claudarama into a military superpower and squash Reese's planet like a moldy orange.

But it turned out his planet, which was called "ReeseRulez," was basically an apocalyptic wasteland, and not in a fun way. Reese was so bad at taking care of it—according to his activity log, he hadn't even visited there in three months—that the whole place had been overrun by some kind of zombie chickens. They'd eaten all the other living things on the planet, and by the time I logged on, they were pecking each other's brains out.

This was mystifying. If Reese wasn't hanging out on his own planet, where was he spending the twelve hours a day he was logged on to MetaWorld?

The answer was Planet Amigo.

REESE

Planet Amigo is this totally beast planet that Akash Gupta, who's an eighth grader at Culvert, built in Conquest mode with his friends.

Akash is crazy good at programming, so Planet Amigo has all kinds of awesome deathmatch arenas and this really cool ranking system where you can get money by winning deathmatches.

Not real money. Planet Amigo money. But that's just as good, because you can use it to build a giant castle for your character to live in, plus an army to protect the castle so nobody burns it down.

And you can use your army to burn down other people's castles. Which is cool. ← also violent/ antisocial

Akash and his friends used to crush everybody in the deathmatches, but I guess they got sick of it, because they're hardly ever on Planet Amigo anymore. Ever since they left, me and Xander have been pwning it. Wyatt's pretty good, too. So's Wenzhi, but his parents only let him play on the weekends. James Mantolini was okay, but he kept griefing everybody, so Akash banned him.

And lately, some Finnish kids have been kicking butt. I'm a little worried about them. They kind of came out of nowhere, and they seem like trouble.

Right now, though, me and Xander pretty much rule the planet. We've got the biggest castles and the most soldiers, and if we wanted to, we could go on a rampage and burn down everybody else's castle.

But then they'd all quit, and there'd be nobody left to beat in the deathmatches. So we let them chill.

CLAUDIA

Basically, Conquest mode is MetaWorld for stupid violent people. I don't know why they don't just call it Stupid Violent mode. But whatever.

Once I realized where Reese was spending all his time, I created an avatar,

"StealthViper999" (because it sounded like a username one of Reese's idiot friends would have), made it look like a musclebound thug (ditto), and logged on to Planet Amigo.

When I spawned, I was all alone in an empty hut. I went outside and found myself in the middle of an apocalyptic wasteland. Unlike ReeseRulez, though, it seemed like an intentional apocalyptic wasteland. There were a few other little huts scattered around, and in the distance I could see a couple of big, castle-type buildings.

Then a musclebound thug (it turned out 99% of everybody on Planet Amigo is a musclebound thug) came out of a hut and walked toward me.

This is when I found out you can chat with other characters in MetaWorld by typing into the box at the bottom of the screen. The conversation started friendly enough:

METAWORLD CHAT LOG

<<GorillaZBT: wut up>>
<<StealthViper999: hello>>

CLAUDIA

But then he pulled a sword, and it got ugly:

METAWORLD CHAT LOG

<<StealthViper999: how do you get a sword?>>
<<GorillaZBT: die n00b!>>

CLAUDIA

He hacked me to death while I was trying to type "what is a n00b?" into the chat box.

I respawned back in my empty hut, and when I went outside again, GorillaZBT was right where I'd left him.

METAWORLD CHAT LOG

```
<<StealthViper999: why did you hack me
to death???>>
<<GorillaZBT: 4 da goldz. duh>>
<<StealthViper999: can you please put
the sword away and have a civilized
conversation?>>
```

CLAUDIA

He put the sword away, and I thought we were making progress.

But then he took out a torch and set fire to my hut.

METAWORLD CHAT LOG

```
<<StealthViper999: Is that a torch?>>
<<StealthViper999: Where do you get
those?>>
<<StealthViper999: WHY ARE YOU SETTING
FIRE TO MY HUT?>>
GorillaZBT burned down StealthViper999's
hut.
<<StealthViper999: You have serious
mental health issues. I think you should
see a psychiatrist.>>
```

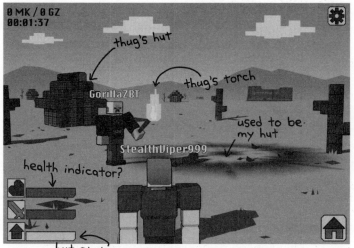

CLAUDIA

Then he hacked me to death with his sword again.

Only this time, I no longer had a hut to respawn in, because he'd burned it down.

So I respawned in some random place in the middle of the wasteland.

Fortunately, GorillaZBT was nowhere in sight.

Unfortunately, other people's avatars were.

And they hacked me to death.

This kept happening until I figured out how to run away. Which was pretty easy, except that I'd be running along and suddenly hit some kind of invisible force field, and a message would pop up that said:

METAWORLD CHAT LOG

Access to DESERT3 denied. Deathmatch in progress. If you wish to participate in a Planet Amigo deathmatch, please sign up in AMIGOCENTRAL.

CLAUDIA

It took me forever—and a ton of reading MetaWorld wikis—to figure out what all that meant.

Basically, if you want to avoid getting hacked to death by everybody you meet on Planet Amigo, you need a castle and an army. But to buy those, you need a lot of goldz, which is Planet Amigo's currency. (I don't know why there's a "z" on the end.)

You can earn goldz by doing something psychotic and/or violent: killing somebody is worth 5 goldz, burning down their hut is worth 10 goldz, etc.

But if you win a deathmatch—which is a big battle where everybody tries to kill each other all at once—you get 1,000 goldz.

So deathmatches are the really important thing on Planet Amigo. A new deathmatch starts every time a dozen players join one, so they're going on all the time.

And Reese must have won TONS of them, because when I finally found his castle, it was absolutely enormous. Also, if I walked too close to it, a bunch of soldiers would come running out, and I'd get a message that said:

METAWORLD CHAT LOG

<<NPC: WARNING—you are trespassing on Skronkmonster's domain. Leave here or die, scum. Have a nice day! :) >>

CLAUDIA

If I didn't turn around and leave after that, Reese's soldiers would hack me to death.

Reese's castle (huge/ugly)

Reese's soldiers (about to hack me to death)

me

This was all pretty daunting. Because it was obvious the only way to take down Reese on Planet Amigo was to win so many deathmatches that I could afford to buy an even bigger army than Reese had.

And when I started entering StealthViper999 in deathmatches, it did not go well.

Here's what the chat log looked like for pretty much every single deathmatch I entered as StealthViper999:

METAWORLD CHAT LOG

```
16 players in FOREST1 Deathmatch on
Planet Amigo.
FOREST1 Deathmatch beginning in 5...
4...
3...
2...
1...
Awrsum killed StealthViper999.
```

CLAUDIA

I died first every time. I was getting killed before I could even take my sword out.

I'm not even sure I had a sword. The whole situation was very confusing.

Maybe if I'd been able to play deathmatches 24/7 for a few weeks, I could've gotten a handle on things. But at this point, I'd spent three straight nights figuring out MetaWorld, and it was starting to mess up my life: my guitar lesson that week was a disaster because I hadn't practiced, I was way behind on my reading response in English, and I'd gotten an 82 on my French test. (If Reese got an 82 on a

French test, he'd be so thrilled he'd tape it to the refrigerator, but for me it was totally shameful.)

So even though I was still desperate for revenge on Reese and Xander, the only way it was going to happen on Planet Amigo was through some kind of divine intervention.

Fortunately, I happen to be close personal friends with the god of Planet Amigo.

CHAPTER 11
(PLANET AMIGO'S)
GOD IS ON MY SIDE

CLAUDIA

Akash Gupta is Planet Amigo's admin, which means he not only created the whole planet, but he can do whatever he wants on it.

So if you want to kill hundreds of soldiers and burn down somebody's giant castle even though you're so clueless you can't figure out which button activates your sword, Akash is a very good person to know.

AKASH GUPTA, admin/god of Planet Amigo

It's called Planet Amigo because me, Dave, and Kwame started planning it in Spanish class last year. Once the younger kids found out about it, the whole thing kind of exploded. Half the people on there now don't even go to Culvert.

Some of them are from Finland, which makes no sense at all. I mean, how did they even find out about it?

Finland

(actually kind of close to Netherlands)

But it's a real hassle to be admin of a planet that big—like, I'm constantly getting messages from sixth graders accusing each other of griefing, so I have to ban them. And once a sixth grader's mom called me because I'd banned her kid for griefing everybody, and I had to be, like, "Look, lady, your son is deranged."

CLAUDIA

Let me guess: James Mantolini?

AKASH

Yeah. There's something wrong with that kid.

Anyway, the crazy thing is, I hardly ever go on Planet Amigo myself anymore. I'm really into BluntForce now, so mostly I hang out on the multiplayer there. MetaWorld seems kind of babyish, to be honest.

But it's still my planet, so I have to admin it. Which means I'm stuck putting all this time into being the god of a place where I don't even hang out. It's pretty annoying.

CLAUDIA

Akash is not only my friend Parvati's older brother, but he's also on Student Government with me. He's the eighth grade class treasurer, and we worked together last year to get Culvert to do a fund-raiser for flood victims in Indonesia. Ever since then, we've been political allies. We're basically as close as a sixth and eighth grader of the opposite sex can be without dating each other.

PARVATI

Ohmygosh, I thought you WERE starting to date for a minute there. That one day after school, you were, like, sitting in the cafeteria together for HOURS.

CLAUDIA

It was a very complicated negotiation. First, I had to convince Akash to help me. He was a little uncomfortable with the idea of abusing his power.

AKASH

I'm a fair god. I don't like to mess with people just because I can. I mean, if one of the Planet Amigo regulars asked me to help him cheat, there's no way I'd do it.

CLAUDIA

Fortunately for me, though, Akash had seen "The Vest Song" on ClickChat.

AKASH

Posting that was way harsh. I could see how you'd want to kick somebody's butt over it. Also, even though I think your brother's pretty cool, I really hate that Xander kid. He's a punk. So I decided it was okay to help you, as long as you were just messing with those two.

CLAUDIA

    What I really wanted was to kill all
of Reese's and Xander's soldiers, burn down
their castles, and make them respawn in the
middle of nowhere with no goldz. But Akash
wouldn't go for it.

AKASH

    It was just way too cruel. I mean,
when I looked at how big Reese and Xander's
castles had gotten, I was pretty shocked.
They must have spent, like, hundreds of
hours of their lives on deathmatches to earn
enough goldz to build those things.

CLAUDIA

    Exactly. So it would have been a very
important lesson in why you SHOULDN'T waste
your life playing deathmatches.

AKASH

    That's a parenting thing. It's not my
job to punish a kid for wasting his life.
    Like I said, I'm a fair god.
    But I was willing to let you mess with
them in the deathmatches. As long as you
weren't too obvious about it.

CLAUDIA

So I asked Akash to give me some kind of shield that'd make me impossible to kill. And lasers to shoot out of my eyes.

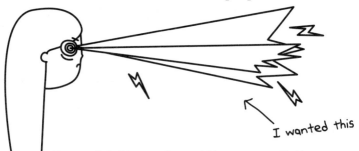

I wanted this

He wouldn't go for either one of those.

AKASH

The thing is, if I made you impossible to kill, every kid in the deathmatch would see it and message-bomb me with complaints.

Plus, lasers in the eyes would have taken me, like, a hundred hours of coding to create. And no offense—I mean, I like you, but I don't "hundred hours of coding" like you.

CLAUDIA

I totally got that. And I didn't want to cause you any trouble. I just wanted to anonymously murder Reese and Xander a couple of hundred times.

AKASH

   Basically, you wanted to be invisible.

CLAUDIA

   Exactly. And when you suggested that,
it made total sense.

← me, being invisible (get it?)

AKASH

   Invisibility was easy. I didn't even
have to code it myself. I found a mod online
and installed it in, like, five minutes.

   But then I had to spend a couple
hours teaching you how to kill people in
deathmatches. Even when you were invisible,
you were pretty hopeless.

CLAUDIA

   I know. I basically suck at video
games. Thank you for being so patient! And
for making me invisible. I REALLY appreciate
it. Seriously, you are a god.

AKASH

   Yes, I am. And you're welcome.

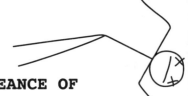

CHAPTER 12
THE TERRIBLE VENGEANCE OF
INVISIBLE DEATH

CLAUDIA

Once Akash set me up with invisibility and taught me some basic killing skills, I deleted StealthViper999—who, I had to admit, was neither stealthy nor viper-like—and created a new avatar, who I called InvisibleDeath.

For obvious reasons.

At this point, it was Friday afternoon, and most weekends, Reese spends every waking minute (when he's not at a soccer game) on MetaWorld. So I was all amped up to get my revenge ASAP.

But that particular Friday, Reese got a 57 on his math test. Even by my brother's incredibly low standards, it was such a bad grade that Ms. Santiago made him take the test home to get it signed by a parent.

REESE

I don't know what the big deal was. A 57's still "Very Good."

CLAUDIA

I should explain about the Culvert Prep grading system. A few years ago, a bunch of parents complained that letter grades were hurting their kids' self-esteem. So now, instead of A, B, C, D, and F, our grading scale is "Amazing," "Spectacular," "Excellent," "Very Good," and "Okay."

Which is totally stupid. Because nothing changed except the names, so if you get a "Very Good" on your report card, your parents have to come in for a special conference with your teacher. And if you get more than one "Okay," they basically tell you to start looking for another school.

Also, I know which parents did the complaining—and I don't want to be catty or name names, but I can tell you the one thing their kids ABSOLUTELY DO NOT NEED is more self-esteem.

Anyway, when Reese brought home his 57 that Friday, Mom and Dad reacted in their usual way, which was to take away all his electronics for a week. Ordinarily, I would have applauded their decision. But in this case, it was a real problem. Not only did it mean I'd have to wait an entire week to get my revenge, but when Reese loses his electronics, he mopes around the house all day and won't stop begging me to play Jenga with him.

Which is particularly annoying, because I am terrible at Jenga.

By Sunday afternoon, I was losing my mind. So I decided to take matters into my own hands. Mom had just left for the airport and yet another business trip, so I went to work on Dad.

Not to brag or anything, but I can be very persuasive. Within five minutes, he was texting Mom:

MOM AND DAD (text messages)

> Claudia says we were too hard on Reese re math test. Bunch of kids complained it was unfair and got worse grades than usual

> Did Reese pay her to say that?

> Don't think so. He is in bedroom playing Jenga by himself. Should I give him electronics back?

Think we need to stick to our guns. Article in NYT said consistency v important in punishing kids

Not sure. Feel like we should let him have laptop at least

You just don't want to play Jenga

Claudia very impassioned about this. Actually kind of touching to see her stick up for brother

felt a little guilty about this

Nice to see she has finally forgiven him...OK. Give him laptop. But first go over math test answers with him

CLAUDIA

Unfortunately, the "go over math test answers" situation turned into a complete nightmare for both Reese and Dad (who is not great at being patient with Reese about his homework), so Reese didn't get his laptop back until it was too late for him to go on MetaWorld that night.

And after Dad told him at dinner that I was the one who'd gotten his punishment

— not a word
(but can't find
real one that fits)

reduced, Reese was so slobberingly thankful
that I thought he might actually try to hug
me. All through Monday, he kept being so
nice to me that—even though the "Vest Song"
nightmare was STILL giving me a stomachache
every time I thought about it—I actually
started to wonder how much I still wanted
revenge.

But then in gym class that afternoon,
I played volleyball against a team with
Xander on it. Right when I was about to
serve (which was traumatic enough, because
I am even worse at volleyball than I am at
Jenga), Xander started singing, "THAT CUTE
LEATHER VEST..."

A bunch of kids laughed, and I turned
bright red and totally whiffed the serve.
That pretty much took care of my second
thoughts. From then on, my one regret
was that I'd only get to stab Xander in
MetaWorld and not in real life.

It was almost nine o'clock that night
before Reese finally finished his homework
and logged on to MetaWorld. At that point,
my InvisibleDeath avatar had been invisibly
hanging out in Planet Amigo's main square

for half an hour, waiting for Reese and Xander to show up and join a deathmatch.

When they finally did, I got excited and scared at the same time—because even though I'd had plenty of practice with Akash, I was still worried I might mess something up.

But it turned out to be easy. I followed them right into a deathmatch, and after it started, all I had to do was run over and stab them a bunch of times.

They both went nuts. It was so hilarious that I saved the screenshots:

METAWORLD CHAT LOG

[Editor's note: Reese is "Skronkmonster," and Xander is "XIzKillinIt."]

```
16 players in DESERT1 Deathmatch on
Planet Amigo.
DESERT1 Deathmatch beginning in 5...
4...
3...
2...
1...
InvisibleDeath killed Skronkmonster.
```

<<Skronkmonster: WAAAAAAA?????>>
Zipthunk killed Badabling.
<<Skronkmonster: whose invisbledeth???
cant even c u>>
<<XIzKillinIt: ha! skronk u suk!>>
InvisibleDeath killed XIzKillinIt.
<<XIzKillinIt: WUTWUT??? NO WAY!!!>>
<<InvisibleDeath: Way.>>
<<Skronkmonster: This is cray>>
<<XIzKillinIt: I M NOT DEAD! THERE WUZ NO
ONE NEAR ME!!!>>
<<InvisibleDeath: You seem pretty dead to
me. Look, there's your corpse!>>
<<Skronkmonster: Invsbledeth where r u?>>
TheMightyFinn killed Blastroy.
<<XIzKillinIt: NOBODY WUZ NEAR ME!!! U R
CHEATING!!!>>
<<InvisibleDeath: and u r dead!>>
Zipthunk killed Trixter.
<<XIzKillinIt: U CANT BE INVISIBLE IN
DEATHMATCH>>
<<InvisibleDeath: I dunno...Kinda seems
like I can.>>
<<Zipthunk: dudes quit clogging feed w ur
whining>>
<<Skronkmonster: X lets go join new match>>

screenshot of first kill

2 MK / 10 GZ
00:32:55

guy stealing sword from dead Reese

Reese corpse

PwnTwn

Skronkmonster

X1zKillinIt

Xander corpse

CLAUDIA

I have to admit my first kill was extremely satisfying. Not only were Reese and Xander freaking out in the chat, but I could hear Reese next door in his bedroom, yelling "WHAAAT?" and "NO WAY!" at his laptop.

The taste of blood made me thirsty for more, so when Reese and Xander logged out to respawn, I went back to Amigo Central and waited for them to reappear and sign up for another deathmatch. When they did, I followed them again:

METAWORLD CHAT LOG

16 players in MURDERTOWN Deathmatch on
Planet Amigo.
MURDERTOWN Deathmatch beginning in 5...
4...
3...
2...
1...
InvisibleDeath killed Skronkmonster.
InvisibleDeath killed XIzKillinIt.
<<Skronkmonster: NOT KEWL!!!!>>
<<XIzKillinIt: WE R GOING 2 KILL U!!!>>
<<InvisibleDeath: I think you are
misunderstanding the situation. It seems
like *I* am the one killing *YOU* :) >>

CLAUDIA

    This went on for a while:

METAWORLD CHAT LOGS

16 players in JUNGLE2 Deathmatch on
Planet Amigo.
JUNGLE2 Deathmatch beginning in 5...
4...

```
3...
2...
1...
InvisibleDeath killed XIzKillinIt.
InvisibleDeath killed Skronkmonster.
<<Skronkmonster: NOT FAIR!!!!>>
<<XIzKillinIt: U WILL DIE!!!>>
<<InvisibleDeath: Technically, yes. I
mean, we're all going to die SOME day.
Right now, though? It's mostly you doing
the dying.>>
```

```
16 players in DARKFOREST Deathmatch on
Planet Amigo.
DARKFOREST Deathmatch beginning in 5...
4...
3...
2...
1...
InvisibleDeath killed XIzKillinIt.
InvisibleDeath killed Skronkmonster.
<<Skronkmonster: Srsly this is NOT KEWL.
Pls leave us alone>>
<<InvisibleDeath: Sorry...!
But no.>>
```

```
16 players in DESERT1 Deathmatch on
Planet Amigo.
DESERT1 Deathmatch beginning in 5...
4...
3...
2...
1...
InvisibleDeath killed Skronkmonster.
InvisibleDeath killed XIzKillinIt.
<<XIzKillinIt: U R GOING 2 GET BANNED BY
ADMIN 4 CHEATING>>
<<InvisibleDeath: U R GOING 2 GET KILLED
BY ME 4 FUN!!!>>
```

CLAUDIA

    Eventually, they gave up:

METAWORLD CHAT LOGS

```
16 players in JUNGLE1 Deathmatch on
Planet Amigo.
JUNGLE1 Deathmatch beginning in 5...
4...
3...
2...
1...
```

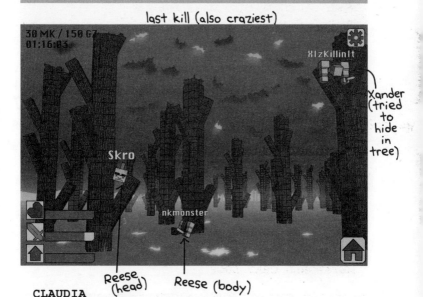

InvisibleDeath killed XIzKillinIt.
InvisibleDeath killed Skronkmonster.
<<Skronkmonster: I quit>>
<<XIzKillinIt: me too this sux>>

last kill (also craziest)

30 MK / 150 GZ
01:16:03

XIzKillinIt

Xander (tried to hide in tree)

Skro

nkmonster

Reese (head)   Reese (body)

CLAUDIA

As far as The War went, this was a
major victory. Basically, I had driven my
enemies from the battlefield in despair. So
you'd think I would've been thrilled.

And at the beginning, I definitely
was. But every time I killed them, it got a
little less fun. It was kind of like eating

ten bowls of ice cream. After a while, it still tastes good, but you're like, "Ugh. Why am I still eating?"

Which was frustrating. All I wanted was some satisfying revenge for the "Vest Song" nightmare. But after I logged off, I didn't feel satisfied. I just felt sort of blech.

So I decided to go next door and check on Reese in person, because I thought maybe if he seemed like he was in horrible anguish, I'd be able to enjoy the moment a little more.

not technically a word (but it should be)

And that's when the whole InvisibleDeath thing started to get weird.

CHAPTER 13
ATTACK OF THE WHINERS

CLAUDIA

When I got to Reese's room, he was hunched over his laptop, banging out a ClickChat message while he yelled at Xander on FaceTime.

I said, "Hey, Reese—what's up?"

And he said something like, "CAN'TTALK PLANETAMIGOMAJORCRISIS!"

I started to say, "Is there anything I can do to help?" But before I could get more than a couple of words out, he went:

"FINNISHHACKERSCAN'TTALKVERYSERIOUSWUAA AAAGH!"

So I decided to back off and watch the situation unfold from a distance.

REESE

Xander and I were mad angry. It's totally illegal to be invisible in a deathmatch! Planet Amigo doesn't even HAVE invisibility!

We figured "InvisibleDeath" must be some kind of hacker, and we should alert

Akash ASAP. He's got a ClickChat account for his admin stuff called "AmigoGod," so we went there to let him know what was up.

CLICKCHAT COMMENTS ON PUBLIC WALL OF "AMIGOGOD"

SKRONKMONSTER AKASH WE HAVE SIRIUS GRIEFER PROBLEM

XlzKillinIt U NEED 2 BAN "INVISIBLEDEATH"

AmigoGod For what?

XlzKillinIt FOR BEING INVISIBLE

SKRONKMONSTER HE IS GRIEFING US IN DETHMATCHS. COULD BE MAJUR AMIGO SECURATY PROBLEM ← *also MAJUR REESE SPELLING PRUBLUM*

AmigoGod Can u please turn off capslock? No need to yell

SKRONKMONSTER Sorry

XlzKillinIt u need 2 ban him now!!!!!!!

SKRONKMONSTER also make sure Invisbledeth hasnt hacked ur whole planet

AmigoGod Who is "invisibledeath?"

SKRONKMONSTER No idea. Think he must b Finnish. When we go on dethmatchs, he kills us right away

AmigoGod Maybe he is just very good at deathmatches

XlzKillinIt hes INVISIBLE!!!!! its illegal!!!!

AmigoGod I will check it out this weekend

XlzKillinIt y not now????

AmigoGod God works in mysterious ways. And has a history test tomorrow

REESE

Xander and I were pretty shocked
that Akash didn't totally freak out about
InvisibleDeath. It seemed like a serious
situation. And when we told everybody about
it the next day at school, it turned out a
ton of other kids were getting griefed by
him on Planet Amigo.

CLAUDIA

This is where it gets crazy. Because
all I did as InvisibleDeath was go on that
one night and kill Xander and Reese a bunch
of times.

That was IT.

But suddenly, InvisibleDeath turned
into this weird boogeyman who got blamed for
everything bad that had ever happened to
anybody in the history of the Internet.

AKASH

I should have told them I'd banned
InvisibleDeath right away. But I had a ton
of stuff going on that week, so I didn't
want to deal. And when I ignored them,
they turned the whole sixth grade into
an angry mob.

CLICKCHAT COMMENTS ON PUBLIC WALL OF "AMIGOGOD"

XlzKillinlt IF U HAV BEEN GRIEFED BY "INVISIBLEDEATH" POST HERE

SKRONKMONSTER He kills people on deathmatches by being invisible!!! It is cheating

XlzKillinlt Plus he stole 5000 goldz from my account it was definately him.

numbah_tehn OMG he's killed me invisiby in deathmatches a bunch of times

bryce_thompson I think he has bn making my computer crash

killrkickr I had goldz stolen from my account to

nightstaker InvisibleDeath hacked my Itunes!!! My dad had 2 change r creditcard no

i_m_ batman_4realz I am InvisibleDeath

numbah_tehn shut up James no u arent

bryce_thompson I bet ID is one of the Finish kids

SKRONKMONSTER I think he is Finnish too

Wenzamura I think my castle got rampaged by ID last week when I was logged off

shabado02 think ID has been hacking me too—my acct is v laggy

i_m_ batman_4realz InvisibleDeath made me poop my pants

numbah_tehn shut up James

killrkickr ID is bad news we should call the cops on him

XlzKillinlt EVRYBODY TELL AKASH HE NEEDZ 2 BAN THIS GRIEFER!!!

CLAUDIA

Reese got so hysterical about InvisibleDeath that he even infected my parents.

MOM AND DAD (text messages)

> Reese says Finnish hackers may have put malware on our home network. You should change all your passwords

> WHAT???

> I don't really understand it either

> Do I seriously have to worry about this?

> Hard to tell. Think so

> I miss the good old days when people just got mugged on the subway

good old days
(lots of muggings)

AKASH

The whole thing was insanely irritating.
I had, like, two tests and a five-page essay
due by Friday, plus my prep class for the
SHSAT, plus play rehearsals. So I was totally
stressed, and suddenly I had these stupid
sixth graders messaging me every five minutes
to tell me I had to ban InvisibleDeath for,
like, destroying their lives. And when I
ignored them online, they started hassling me
in the hallways at school.

It was like a plague of idiots in
soccer jerseys.

CLAUDIA

I'm sorry. It's my fault they all
freaked out on you.

AKASH

I guess so. But you weren't the one I was mad at. It was them.

Mostly because it was the principle of the thing. Like, I built that whole planet! They've been playing on it for free since January, not a single one of them has ever even, like, thanked me for it—and then suddenly, they start ordering me around like I'm their slave!

And some of them had SERIOUSLY bad attitudes. Your brother was just kind of, like, whatever. Low-grade annoying. But that Xander punk kept going *[EXTREMELY STUPID PERSON VOICE]*, "Yo, AK-Fiddy-Seven, you gots to lock dat ish down!"

Who even talks like that?

And he wasn't even saying it right. "Fiddy-Seven" is "FIFTY-seven." But it's an AK-FORTY-seven.

What an idiot. Is it true his ancestors were on the *Mayflower*?

CLAUDIA

I think so.

AKASH

Wow. That is just sad. America's really gone downhill in the last 400 years.

And he kept whining about how somebody stole 5,000 goldz from his account! Which is totally impossible. And it's not even real money! Hello? I invented it! IT'S WORTHLESS!

The last straw was when Xander started texting me at eleven o'clock at night. I got so mad, I was like, "I should just blow up Planet Amigo."

That's when I decided to stop being a fair god and start being a vengeful god.

CLAUDIA

Akash got so mad at Reese and Xander that he told me to do what I'd wanted from the beginning—which was to destroy everything they owned on Planet Amigo.

At first, I wasn't sure if I was up for it. Killing them in the deathmatches hadn't been nearly as satisfying as I'd expected, and I still couldn't figure out why.

But I thought about it for a while, and I decided the problem was that the deathmatches weren't real enough. Every time

I'd killed Reese and Xander, they'd just respawned back in their giant castles. They didn't even lose any goldz. Other than their paranoid freakout over InvisibleDeath, once they logged off, it was like nothing had ever happened.

Meanwhile, I was still feeling so much leftover trauma from the "Vest Song" horror show that I was convinced it'd take me years of therapy to get over it.

So I figured the only way to guarantee justice had been served was to COMPLETELY ANNIHILATE Reese and Xander—to kill all their soldiers, burn down their castles, and leave them with nothing but bitter tears to show for the hundreds of hours they'd spent building their stupid little Amigo empires.

I realize that sounds a little psycho. But the thing is, after you've been in a war for a while, it messes with your head. If you're not careful, you can wind up convincing yourself that something totally psycho is not just normal, but actually a smart thing to do.

Plus, god told me to do it. So I figured it must be okay. (Amigo god, NOT real God)

CHAPTER 14
THE THURSDAY
NIGHT MASSACRE

CLAUDIA

First, Akash fixed it so InvisibleDeath was impossible to kill. Then he gave me 1,000 firebombs and a shotgun with unlimited ammunition.

I asked for lasers I could shoot out of my eyes, but he still wouldn't go for it.

AKASH

I don't know why you were so hung up on lasers. Everybody else on Planet Amigo just has swords and arrows, so the firebombs and the shotgun were more than enough to achieve tactical dominance.

CLAUDIA

Whatever. I wanted to make sure Reese and Xander were both online to see me wipe them out, so I created an InvisibleDeath ClickChat account and went looking for them on AmigoGod's wall:

CLICKCHAT COMMENTS ON PUBLIC WALL OF "AMIGOGOD"

XlzKillinIt yo AK-57 wut up wit InvisibleDeath? Did u ban him??

InvisibleDeath Did someone mention my name?

XlzKillinIt OMG U R DEAD!!!

InvisibleDeath Summon the one you call "Skronkmonster." I have a proposition for you.

XlzKillinIt hang on I texted him hes coming

XlzKillinIt And u better give back my 5000 goldz or I will get cops involved

SKRONKMONSTER Im here. WHO R U???

InvisibleDeath I am Death, come to deliver my final judgment. How does 8pm tonight sound?

SKRONKMONSTER What do u mean?

InvisibleDeath Meet me in front of Skronkmonster's Planet Amigo castle at 8pm. Bring all your soldiers.

SKRONKMONSTER first tell us who u r

XlzKillinIt first give me my 5000 goldz back

InvisibleDeath Xander, please shut up about your 5000 goldz. I did not take it.

XlzKillinIt HOW DO U NO MY NAME????

InvisibleDeath I know everything. Plus it's on your home page, idiot. Are you going to meet me tonight or not?

XlzKillinIt WE CANT FIGHT U BC U CHEAT

InvisibleDeath how do I cheat?

XlzKillinIt U R INVISIBLE DUUUUH

InvisibleDeath I will cast aside my cloak of invisibility and show myself to you at 8pm tonight in front of Skronkmonster's castle. BE THERE.
SKRONKMONSTER 8pm ur time or ours?
InvisibleDeath What do you mean?
SKRONKMONSTER arent u in Finland
InvisibleDeath No. 8pm NYC time
SKRONKMONSTER ok

REESE

After InvisibleDeath challenged us on ClickChat, me and Xander went into total war mode. We spent all the goldz we had buying more soldiers and upgrading their weapons, so by eight o'clock, we had almost 600 soldiers with plate armor and platinum swords.

Then we waited outside my castle to kick InvisibleDeath's butt.

CLAUDIA

MetaWorld has a gazillion options for avatars, so it took me a while to decide what InvisibleDeath should look like. Eventually, I went with a little girl in blond pigtails, a blue dress with yellow polka dots, and big dark eyes that made me look like a Japanese cartoon character.

I looked totally cute. I was so tiny my shotgun was twice as big as me. my avatar (shotgun not pictured)

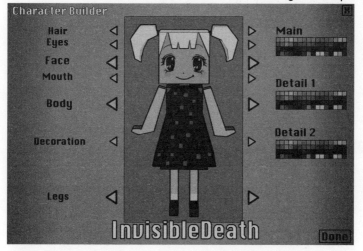

It seemed like the best way to go, because I figured the more teensy and harmless I looked, the more devastating it'd be for Reese and Xander when my cute little girl slaughtered their armies and burned down their castles.

Here's how they reacted when I showed up a couple minutes after 8:00. Their army was so big it looked like a forest of heads behind them:

METAWORLD CHAT LOG

<<Skronkmonster: r u invisibledeath?>>
<<XIzKillinIt: HAHAHAHA U LOOK
RIDICULUS>>
<<Skronkmonster: u look like a 6 yr
old>>
<<InvisibleDeath: Maybe I am.>>
<<XIzKillinIt: U R DOOMED>>
<<Skronkmonster: You dont even have
any solders!>>
<<XIzKillinIt: THIS WILL HURT U A
LOOOOOT>>
<<Skronkmonster: wait is that a gun?>>
<<InvisibleDeath: Why, yes it is! Do
you like my gun?>>
<<XIzKillinIt: GUNS R ILLEGAL ON
AMIGO>>
<<Skronkmonster: srsly u cant have one>>
<<InvisibleDeath: And yet...I do.>>
<<XIzKillinIt: PUT IT AWAY LITTLE GURL>>
<<InvisibleDeath: Hmmm. My gun has
decided it doesn't like you.>>
InvisibleDeath killed XIzKillinIt.
<<Skronkmonster: omg!>>
InvisibleDeath killed Skronkmonster.

CLAUDIA

Shooting them that first time turned out to be almost as satisfying as the first deathmatch kill. But I didn't have much time to enjoy it, because right after I shot Reese and Xander, their corpses dissolved, and while they were respawning back in their castles, their whole army attacked me at once.

Seeing all 600 or whatever soldiers draw their swords at the same time actually looked really cool, although it scared me so much my heart started to thump.

Then they all ran at me, and I had to start shooting.

It got crazy fast. My whole monitor filled up with soldiers. They kept hacking at me with their swords, but Akash had made me invincible, so it didn't do any damage. And they were so close I didn't even have to aim—all I had to do was keep pressing "F" to fire and "R" to reload.

Little red pixels of blood were flying everywhere, and the corpses started piling up so high that I had to move backwards to make room for more.

screenshot from mid-massacre (huge mess)

I think I must have been hitting
the fire and reload buttons too hard or
something, because pretty quickly, my
forearms started to hurt.

Every ten seconds or so, the chat log
ran a tally of how many soldiers I'd just
killed. I was up to about 100 by the time
Reese and Xander came back.

I couldn't see them, because my
screen was full of soldiers and pixel
blood. But they started going nuts on
the chat:

METAWORLD CHAT LOG

```
InvisibleDeath killed 21 Skronkmonster
NPCs.
InvisibleDeath killed 14 XIzKillinIt NPCs.
<<Skronkmonster: U CAN'T DO THIS>>
<<Skronkmonster: NO GUNZ ALLOWED>>
<<Skronkmonster: STOP>>
<<Skronkmonster: NOW>>
<<Skronkmonster: PLEASE>>
InvisibleDeath killed 17 Skronkmonster
NPCs.
InvisibleDeath killed 24 XIzKillinIt NPCs.
```

<<Skronkmonster: SRSLY THIS IS NOT
RIGHT>>
<<XIzKillinIt: yo I m back>>
<<Skronkmonster: we have 2 stop him hes
killing all our soldiers>>
<<XIzKillinIt: I hav plan hit me on
FaceTime>>
<<Skronkmonster: ok>>
InvisibleDeath killed 32 Skronkmonster
NPCs.

CLAUDIA

A few seconds later, I heard Reese
through the bedroom wall, yelling back and
forth with Xander on FaceTime. Xander's plan
must have been to circle around and attack
me from behind.

Which was brilliant.

(I'm being sarcastic. All I had to do
was turn around to kill them.)

METAWORLD CHAT LOG

<<Skronkmonster: Y R U NOT DEAD?? I HIT
YOU 20 TIMES>>
InvisibleDeath killed XIzKillinIt.
InvisibleDeath killed Skronkmonster.

CLAUDIA

By now, my wrist was seriously cramping up from hitting the buttons over and over again, and I started to worry that if I had to shoot all 600 soldiers, I was going to get carpal tunnel syndrome and be crippled for life.

Fortunately, just then I remembered I had firebombs. I started chucking them at the soldiers, and that took it to a WHOLE other level.

METAWORLD CHAT LOG

```
InvisibleDeath killed 42 Skronkmonster
NPCs.
InvisibleDeath killed 31 XIzKillinIt
NPCs.
<<Skronkmonster: NOOOOOOOOOO>>
<<XIzKillinIt: NOOOOT KEEEEWWWL!!!>>
<<Skronkmonster: TRUCE!>>
<<Skronkmonster: PLEASE!>>
InvisibleDeath killed 37 Skronkmonster
NPCs.
InvisibleDeath killed 54 XIzKillinIt
NPCs.
```

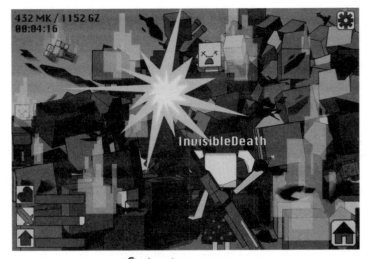

Firebombs = crazy

CLAUDIA

I could hear Reese in his bedroom, yelling "NOO!" and "I CAN'T BELIEVE THIS!"

Then Xander quit.

METAWORLD CHAT LOG

<<XIzKillinIt: dude I have 2 log off>>
<<Skronkmonster: WHAT???>>
InvisibleDeath killed 26 Skronkmonster NPCs.
InvisibleDeath killed 31 XIzKillinIt NPCs.
<<XIzKillinIt: I hav homewrk>>

```
<<Skronkmonster: U NEVER DO UR
HOMEWORK>>
XIzKillinIt has logged off.
<<Skronkmonster: XANDER NO!!!!>>
InvisibleDeath killed 53 Skronkmonster
NPCs.
```

REESE

Sometimes, it's not that cool being Xander's friend. This was one of those times.

I was totally (skronked) that he quit on me like that.

not a real word (but probably means "very sad")

CLAUDIA

Xander must have quit FaceTime, too, because I heard Reese yell "XANDER?" a few times, like he couldn't figure out where he went.

Then he stopped yelling and started moaning—loud, wailing moans, like a dying cow.

To be honest, it was kind of upsetting. By now, Reese's soldiers were all dead, so I started lobbing firebombs at his castle.

METAWORLD CHAT LOG

<<Skronkmonster: CAN WE HAVE A TRUCE??>>
<<Skronkmonster: PLEASE DO NOT BURN DOWN
MY CASTLE!!!>>
<<Skronkmonster: I WILL PAY YOU
GOLDZ!!!>>

CLAUDIA

At this point, Reese's begging and moaning was starting to get to me. I didn't even want to taunt him anymore.

So I shot his avatar to put him out of his misery.

METAWORLD CHAT LOG

<<Skronkmonster: PLEEEEEASE!!!>>
InvisibleDeath **killed** Skronkmonster.

CLAUDIA

After that, he didn't come back. But his castle was so big that it took another couple of dozen firebombs to burn it down.

I could still hear Reese moaning in the next room. Then Mom (who was home early that night) must have gone in to see what was wrong, because the moaning stopped, and I started to hear muffled voices. I couldn't make out what they were saying, partly because I had to keep banging on the "T" button to throw the firebombs. But I could tell Reese was upset, and Mom was trying to cheer him up.

By now, I felt totally gross. It turns out killing a few hundred soldiers, even if they're totally fake and look like Legos—and even if it's totally justifiable revenge—is even less emotionally fun than shooting somebody's avatar seventeen times in a deathmatch.

Burning down a giant castle feels kind of horrible, too. Especially when it's your twin brother's castle, and he won't quit moaning about it in the next room.

And it's making practically your whole arm cramp up, so it's physically painful on top of everything else.

But I am not the kind of person who quits a job without finishing it. I kept lobbing firebombs until I got the message:

METAWORLD CHAT LOG

> InvisibleDeath **burned down** Skronkmonster's castle.

CLAUDIA

The muffled talking in the next bedroom had stopped by then. It was so quiet I could hear the traffic whoosh by on West End Avenue.

I sat there for a while, staring at the screen. All the soldiers' corpses and blood had dissolved. There was nothing left of Reese's Planet Amigo empire except the scorched hole where his castle used to be.

The more I stared at it, the more disgusting I felt.

So I went to the kitchen to get a toaster pastry. Because when I am feeling down, a toaster pastry usually helps.

Reese and Mom were sitting at the kitchen table. Reese had this incredibly sad look on his face, like he'd just finished crying. Mom was rubbing his back and saying, "Well, sweetie, isn't that just what happens in video games?"

And in this tiny, trembly voice, Reese said, "You don't understand. I worked SO HARD on it! And it's GONE. 'Cause he CHEATED...."

Then he started to cry a little.

It was awful. This was supposed to be my moment of triumph. I'd won The War!

Except I didn't feel triumphant at all. I felt disgusting.

I went to the cabinet and got out a box of toaster pastries. There was only one left.

"Hey, Reese," I said. "Do you want the last toaster pastry?"

And he snuffled and said, "No. You can have it."

"I think it's yours, though," I said.

"That's okay," he said. "You can have it anyway."

That made me feel even worse.

Because even though my brother can be incredibly annoying, he is basically a good person. And even though making him miserable was perfectly fair considering what he and Xander had done to me, that didn't mean it was right.

Instead of eating the toaster pastry, I went to my room and messaged Akash:

CLAUDIA AND AKASH (ClickChat Direct Messenger)

Is there any way to put Reese's castle and soldiers back like they were?

Did you destroy them all?

Yes but now I feel horrible

Xander's, too?

No. He logged off before I could finish

Destroy Xander and I will
see what I can do

Ugh. Seriously?

Yes seriously. You have to
destroy Xander's castle

I just want to forget the
whole thing

We had a deal. You promised to
destroy them both

But it turns out destroying things is
totally gross. Can't you please just
put it all back?

Sorry. You make a deal with
the devil, you suffer the
consequences

THE DEVIL??? I thought you
were god

Surprise! I am both

AKASH

The truth is, I was ALWAYS going to put everything back the way it was.

CLAUDIA

Seriously?

AKASH

Of course! I am a fair god. And the players on my server are my children. Even the punks.

So when I made you impossible to kill, I also programmed it so in 48 hours, anything you'd killed or burned down would automatically restore.

CLAUDIA

WHY DIDN'T YOU TELL ME THAT? I wouldn't have had to spend all that time feeling awful!

AKASH

But you NEEDED to feel awful. So you could see for yourself that mindless destruction and revenge don't solve anything. And your brother and that idiot

Xander had to learn to appreciate what
they've got, even if it's just on a server.
And that karma exists for them—so when
they mess with somebody online, they'll get
messed with right back.

Basically, all three of you needed to
learn a whole buttload of life lessons.

CLAUDIA

I guess you're right....You're very
wise, you know that?

AKASH

Well, I AM god. ←

not literally.
Just on
Planet Amigo.

CLAUDIA

Good point.

I definitely learned my lesson. The
War made me psycho in a way I'm not
proud of.

I am NEVER going to war with anybody
again. Unless they completely deserve it.

And even then, I'll assemble a
coalition first (either through the United
Nations, or the people who sit at my lunch
table, or whatever) so I have allies who can

check my behavior and make sure I don't get psycho.

This was a very important lesson. And I'd like to point out that I learned it EVEN BEFORE the whole situation blew up in my face in a spectacularly horrible way.

CHAPTER 15
THE FRIDAY MORNING CATASTROPHE

CLAUDIA

I was too burned out to go back on MetaWorld that night. Instead, I went to bed and set my alarm to get up half an hour early so I could burn down Xander's castle before school.

When I opened my computer the next morning, I checked ClickChat first. Because it's basically a habit.

Sophie was online, asking whether she should wear her new five-toed socks to school:

CLICKCHAT COMMENTS ON PUBLIC WALL OF "SOPHIE_K_NYC"

sophie_k_nyc is it cold enough to wear these yet?

CLAUDIA

I typed an answer, and just when I was about to hit return, a comment from Xander popped up on Sophie's wall.

And because the horrible regret I felt about destroying my brother's castle absolutely DID NOT INCLUDE Xander, who is completely vile and deserves whatever pain he gets, I decided that as long as he was on ClickChat, I'd spend a little quality time taunting him.

So I hit return on my comment to Sophie really fast, then switched from my usual "claudaroo" account to my "InvisibleDeath" account.

Except that I'd never switched back after my exchange with Xander and Reese the day before. So this is what wound up on Sophie's wall:

<< 202 >>

CLICKCHAT COMMENTS ON PUBLIC WALL OF
"SOPHIE_K_NYC"

Parvanana Yah go for it

XIzKillinIt who cares about yr rank sweaty toes

sophie_k_nyc Xander do I have 2 block u again?

InvisibleDeath OMG totally cute! wear them!

sophie_k_nyc ummm...who is "InvisibleDeath"?

XIzKillinIt WUUUUUUUUT?????

CLAUDIA

Because I'd switched accounts so fast,
I didn't see Sophie's and Xander's replies.

So I didn't realize I was using the
wrong account...and what I posted on
Xander's wall was:

CLICKCHAT COMMENT ON PUBLIC WALL OF
"XIZKILLINIT"

claudaroo I'm coming for you, Xander. I'm coming to destroy
you. I will burn down your home and slaughter everyone in it and
leave you with nothing but the bitter memory of how you ran
like a coward and abandoned your friend. Did you think running
away could save you? Did you think I would forget? I know
where you live, Xander. Enjoy this day. It will be your last. YOU
ARE GOING TO DIE IN THE FLAMES OF MY VENGEANCE.

CLAUDIA

I spent so long writing the perfect taunt that I basically ran out of time to burn down Xander's castle, and as soon as I hit return, I had to log off and get ready for school.

Which is why I also missed seeing Xander's reply:

CLICKCHAT COMMENT ON PUBLIC WALL OF "XIZKILLINIT"

XIzKillinIt **CLAUDIA U R SOOOO BUSTED!!! #ZeroTolaranceBaby**

CLAUDIA

I was in math class when Mrs. Bevan came for me.

JOANNA BEVAN, Vice Principal, Culvert Prep Middle School

I know it seems excessive. But like I said: that's the problem with a "zero tolerance" policy. It ties my hands as an administrator.

If there is literally "zero" tolerance for cyberbullying, when someone presents me with evidence of an incident, I can't take the source, or the context, or any nuance into consideration.

I just have to lay down the law.

So when Xander Billington showed me that printout from his ClickChat account, I didn't have a choice.

I had to suspend you.

I'm sorry, Claudia.

CLAUDIA

I'm sorry, too, Mrs. Bevan.

This has been a very valuable learning experience.

MOM AND DAD (text messages)

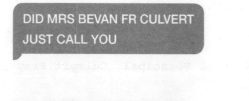

DID MRS BEVAN FR CULVERT JUST CALL YOU

No. Why?

CLAUDIA GOT SUSPENDED FROM SCHOOL

You mean Reese

NO. CLAUDIA

OMG WHAT FOR

CYBERBULLYING XANDER
BILLINGTON

I no longer understand how the
world works

CHAPTER 16
PEACE IN OUR TIME

CLAUDIA

Not only did I get a one-day suspension.

Not only did Mrs. Bevan call my parents and get me in crazy trouble at home.

But now I have a police record.

Because according to Culvert Prep's zero tolerance policy, the school has to report any threats of physical violence to the police. And according to Xander, what I wrote on his wall was a threat of physical violence.

Even though it was actually just a threat of DIGITAL violence.

And even though, thanks to Akash, it was only going to be temporary.

And even though I never even followed through on it.

Because, really, what was the point? I'd had enough. I was done.

And when Akash's program automatically restored Reese's castle and soldiers, my brother was so happy he ran through the

apartment yelling "SKA-DA-BOOOSH!" and
"HIBBITY ZIB-ZAB!"

Which I guess for Reese was like the
equivalent of when World War II ended, and
everybody went to Times Square to make out
with sailors.

The War was over.

I lost.

I just wish there was some kind of program Akash could run on my life to erase the whole thing so it never happened.

REESE

I don't get it. If you wish it never happened, why are you writing a whole book about it?

CLAUDIA

Because people have to understand it was your fault!

REESE

But it wasn't my fault.

CLAUDIA

Yes, it was!

REESE

No, it wasn't. Read the book if you don't believe me.

CLAUDIA

Did YOU read the book?

REESE

No.

Sorry. I'm going to! Eventually.

But I don't HAVE to read it. I was there! Starting with the toaster pastry—

CLAUDIA

It doesn't—!

It's not—!

Look...

I HAVE to be able to explain...why my police record...WASN'T MY FAULT.

REESE

Explain to who?

CLAUDIA

People!

REESE

What people?

CLAUDIA

People in the future!

REESE

I have no idea what you're talking about.

CLAUDIA

Of course you don't! Because all you want to do with your life is be a professional soccer player!

And nobody cares if a soccer player has a police record. They probably ALL do!

But I CAN'T HAVE ONE!

REESE

Why not?

CLAUDIA

Because...just forget it.

REESE

Is this about you wanting to be president?

CLAUDIA

No!

REESE

Really?

REALLY?

CLAUDIA

Okay, yes.

<< 211 >>

Do NOT make fun of me! Just because I
set very high goals for myself—

REESE

I'm not making fun of you! I think it's
totally cool.

CLAUDIA

Really?

REESE

Yeah! Do you know how awesome it'd be
for me if my sister was the president? I
could, like, hang out at the White House
whenever I wanted—

CLAUDIA

I don't know about "whenever"—

REESE

Oh, come on!

CLAUDIA

Definitely sometimes. Just not, like,
every day.

Reese can hang out here (but only sometimes)

But that's the thing—if I have a police record, it'll come out during, like, the New Hampshire primary, and I'll never get elected!

REESE

Are you kidding? By the time you're old enough to be president? EVERYBODY will have a police record.

CLAUDIA

That is ridiculous.

REESE

No, seriously. I heard, like, America puts more people in jail than any other country in the world. So we're basically ALL going to jail at some point.

CLAUDIA

You realize that's completely insane, right?

REESE

Whatever. You'll get elected anyway! You're totally brilliant. You're, like, the smartest person in our class.

CLAUDIA

You really think that?

REESE

Duh! It's obvious.

CLAUDIA

Ohmygosh...That is such a nice thing to say.

REESE

Well, I mean it. Just because I hate you doesn't mean you're not awesome.

CLAUDIA

Thanks, Reese.

You're a really nice person, you know that?

REESE

I dunno. I guess so.

CLAUDIA

I mean, you're so nice it's actually hard to be in a war with you. It's like being in a war with a golden retriever.

very hard to go to war against this

Ugh! What a mess. I never should've put that fish in your backpack.

REESE

Well, look on the bright side—if you hadn't, you never would've found out Jens likes you.

CLAUDIA

WHAT?????!!!!!!

REESE

You didn't know that?

CLAUDIA

NO, I DID NOT. TELL ME EVERYTHING.

REESE

Well, after that whole "Vest Song" thing—seriously, I am SO sorry—

CLAUDIA

It's fine! Just keep going!

REESE

Well, a bunch of us were ripping on him about it at practice. And he was, like, "I don't care. Your sister is cute. I HOPE that song was about me."

CLAUDIA

OHMYGOSHYOU'RETOTALLYLYINGHEDIDNOTSAY THAT!

REESE

No, he did. He said it. Seriously.

CLAUDIA

Why did I not know this???!!! Why didn't you tell me?

REESE

Because you weren't talking to me. And
by the time you started again, it was, like,
weeks later. And I just kind of forgot.

CLAUDIA

You are the greatest brother ever.

REESE

You're just saying that.

CLAUDIA

True. But I sort of mean it, too. I
gotta go tell Sophie. This is CRAZY!

REESE

So we're cool, right? With this war
thing? Truce?

CLAUDIA

Truce. Totally.

EPILOGUE
(i.e., the very, very end)

CLAUDIA

There are definitely a lot of very important lessons to be learned from The War.

But I can't think of what they are right now, and I have to go meet Sophie and Carmen at Starbucks in ten minutes to strategize the best way to handle the Jens situation.

So I will try to sum up quickly:

If you absolutely have to get involved in a war, try not to let it be with your twin brother. Because even if you win, you will feel totally gross—and when it's all over, you'll realize that even though he can be a complete idiot and has terrible taste in friends, deep down he's a good person who probably cares about you. And maybe you should try to look out for him, too.

Fortunately, except for my police record (and Sophie thinks there might not even BE a police record, because Mrs. Bevan was probably bluffing, like when Mr. Greenwald tells us he's going to email our

parents for talking in science class but
then never does), nothing permanently bad
happened as a result of this particular War.

Now that Reese and I have made peace,
it's almost like it never even happened.

Almost.

MOM AND DAD (text messages)

My winter coat smells like a dead fish

Mine too

THE
END

SPECIAL THANKS

Nina Lipkind, Gage Jayko, Brittney Morello, Matt Berenson, Ronin Rodkey, Rahm Rodkey, Michael Frank, Amanda Newman, Lily Feldman, Amy Giddon, the Newman-Corré Family, Lisa Clark, Liz Casal, Andrea Spooner, Deirdre Jones, and Josh Getzler.

PHOTO CREDITS

All photographs are copyright © 2015 by Geoff Rodkey except for the following, reprinted with permission:

p. 1: United States Navy
p. 2: United Kingdom Government
pp. 8, 14, 15, 32, 69: Ronin Rodkey
pp. 21, 152: Ekler Vector/Shutterstock.com
p. 25: Amanda Newman
p. 31: Curtis Brown Photography
p. 36: Hulton Royals Collection/Getty Images
p. 42: antpun/Shutterstock.com
p. 51: Elizabeth Newman-Corré
p. 59: Erin Simon Berenson
p. 61: Stephen Rees/Shutterstock.com
p. 68: Currier & Ives N.Y.
p. 79: Express Newspapers/Getty Images
p. 84: cbpix/Shutterstock.com
p. 94: khuruzero/Shutterstock.com
p. 108: Vicke Andren
p. 110, top: Marsan/Shutterstock.com
p. 110, middle: Firma V/Shutterstock.com
p. 110, bottom: Tooykrub/Shutterstock.com
p. 112: smuay/Shutterstock.com
p. 152: Ekler Vector/Shutterstock.com
p. 176: National Archives and Records Administration (USA)
p. 201: Nina Lipkind
p. 208: Alfred Eisenstaedt/Getty Images
p. 213: Natalia Pushchina/Shutterstock.com
p. 215: Mat Hayward/Shutterstock.com

ILLUSTRATION CREDITS

Liz Casal: pp. iii, 1, 3, 6, 14, 17, 18, 22, 29, 35, 38, 54, 65, 82, 89, 96, 105, 118, 119, 134, 151, 156, 158, 171, 180, 201, 207, 219
Lisa Clark: pp. 138, 142, 145, 148, 165, 169, 183, 185, 186, 190, 194
Chris Goodhue: p. 7

COMING SOON!

To a bookstore and/or library and/or e-reader device thing near you!

THE TAPPER TWINS TEAR UP NEW YORK

It is three times funnier and five times crazier than THE TAPPER TWINS GO TO WAR! (Seriously.)

Turn this page for a sneak preview!

(and/or swipe left on e-reader thing)

PROLOGUE

CLAUDIA

This is the official history of the First Annual Culvert Prep Middle School Scavenger Hunt For Charity.

I am writing it because there is a WHOLE lot of bad information out there about what happened. Mostly because of that stupid article in the *New York Star*.

— NOT TRUE

SCHOOLKID SCAVENGERS RUN RIOT
Private School Kids, Parents In Fundraiser Fracas

(kind of true)

Which was almost completely not true. At no point did anybody involved in the hunt "run riot."

Except possibly for a couple of minutes at the end. But I can explain that.

And I'll admit that what happened was technically a "fracas." But since almost nobody has any idea what that word means, it's kind of ridiculous to put it in a headline.

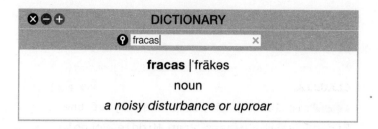

fracas |ˈfrākəs

noun

a noisy disturbance or uproar

Also, some of the things that happened with my brother Reese's team were definitely not good. Or legal.

But overall, the scavenger hunt was a HUGE SUCCESS. We raised $8,748.75 for the Manhattan Food Bank, which is TOTALLY AMAZING. A LOT of hungry people got to eat decent meals thanks to our scavenger hunt.

Not that you'd know any of this from reading the stupid *New York Star*.

Which, again, is why I'm writing this history, based on interviews with everyone involved. Because as the person who not *except people who wouldn't talk to me* only had the idea for the hunt, but also organized it, all this misinformation has been very painful and frustrating.

The fact that there will not be a Second Annual Scavenger Hunt—because Vice Principal Bevan has banned them forever—is also very frustrating.

And honestly, I think Mrs. Bevan overreacted. Nobody actually filed a lawsuit. Those were just empty threats.

(so far)

REESE

All I can say is, none of the bad stuff that happened on our team was my fault. Most of the laws we broke, I didn't even know were laws. So those shouldn't count.

And none of it would've happened in the first place if Dad had done a better job of being our team chaperone.

I don't want to throw Dad under the bus or anything. But that was pretty much the whole problem right there.

Mom's still really mad at him for it.

MOM AND DAD (Text messages copied from Mom's phone)

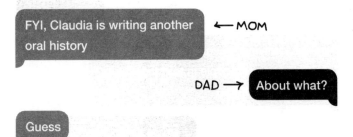

FYI, Claudia is writing another oral history ←— MOM

DAD —→ About what?

Guess

I know you are. And I forgive you

so you won't let her use texts, right?

right?

honey?

no comment

Thanks, Mom!

CHAPTER 1
I HAVE AN EXCELLENT IDEA
(WITH A LITTLE HELP FROM
MY BROTHER)

CLAUDIA

I came up with the idea for the scavenger hunt while taking the M79 bus across Central Park to school.

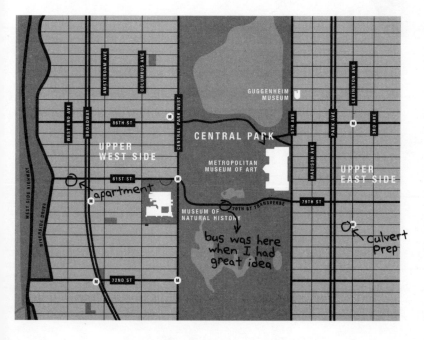

REESE

You didn't come up with it! It was
MY idea!

You just ripped it off. And you never
once gave me credit!

CLAUDIA

Do you seriously want credit for it?
After everything that happened?

REESE

Oh, yeah...Good point. Never mind.

CLAUDIA

By the way, for anyone who doesn't
already know, Reese and I are twins.

Which is weird. Because we are not
twin-like at all. In fact, we are VERY
different.

I don't want to get into HOW we're
different, because I believe every person
is special and unique—and if you put a
label on someone, it's like forcing
them into a tiny box where they have
no room to move and can't just be
themselves.

Which, obviously, is not cool.

if we were pets, I would be:

and Reese would be:

Although if I absolutely HAD to put labels on us, I would be The Smart One.

And Reese would be The Sporty One.

Or possibly The Smelly One.

Or maybe even The One Who Wastes His Life Playing Video Games While His Sister Is Busy Trying To Make The World A Better Place.

See what I mean about labels? They are very unfair.

Even when they're true.

Back to the M79 bus.

M79 bus = crazy slow
(but faster than walking)
(but not by much)

Reese and I were sitting together, and I was writing a speech for Student Government about my proposal to do a fund-raiser for the Manhattan Food Bank.

The fact that some people in New York City don't have enough food to eat REALLY bothers me. Especially when you consider how well off a lot of families at Culvert Prep are. It just seems completely unfair and wrong that kids could go hungry in one part of the city while people like Athena Cohen have so much money they can fly to Bermuda every weekend on a private jet.

And as president, I'd decided I should do something about this.

REESE

You realize you're only president of the sixth grade, right?

Like, you're not president of the whole city?

CLAUDIA

Okay, A) Duh.

B) New York City has a MAYOR, not a president.

NYC mayor lives here
(almost as nice as White House)
(but hard to get good pic due to trees/fence)

And C) have you ever heard the term "Think globally, act locally"?

REESE

Maybe. Was that in a Burger King commercial?

CLAUDIA

I am almost completely sure it wasn't.

REESE

Oh. Then no.

CLAUDIA

That is just sad, Reese. Seriously.

Back to the bus. I was working on my speech. And Reese was babbling about some MetaWorld thing.

REESE

    MetaWorld is, like, the greatest video game in the history of the universe. It's not even one game. It's more <u>like fifty</u> different games all skrudged together. *not an actual word*

    And one of them is MetaHunt, which is this super-massive scavenger hunt. Only it's MUCH cooler than a regular scavenger hunt, because you can kill other players and take all their stuff. So if you kill enough people, you don't even have to find any of the stuff yourself.

MetaHunt looks like this:

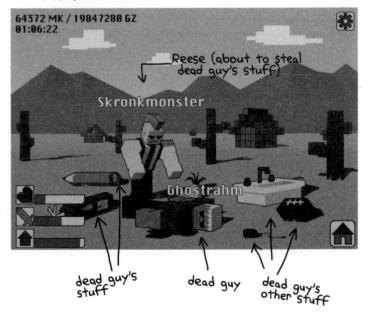

64372 MK / 19847280 GZ
01:06:22

Reese (about to steal dead guy's stuff)

Skronkmonster

Ghostrahm

dead guy's stuff

dead guy

dead guy's other stuff

I'd been playing a ton of MetaHunt, and it got me thinking how awesome it'd be to do a scavenger hunt for real all over New York City.

We couldn't, like, actually kill each other. But it'd still be cool.

So when Claudia was like, "Shut up, Reese! I'm writing my Student Government speech!"

I was like, "You should have the SG do a scavenger hunt! For the whole school!"

And Claudia was, like, "That is the DUMBEST idea—heeeeey, wait a minute..."

CLAUDIA

And that's basically how it all started.

Read the rest of the story in
THE TAPPER TWINS
TEAR UP NEW YORK

Coming Fall 2015!

ABOUT THE AUTHOR

Geoff Rodkey is best known as the screenwriter of the hit films *Daddy Day Care*, *RV*, and the Disney Channel's *Good Luck Charlie, It's Christmas*. The author of the acclaimed middle-grade adventure-comedy trilogy *The Chronicles of Egg*, he's also written for the educational video game *Where in the World Is Carmen Sandiego?*, the non-educational MTV series *Beavis and Butt-Head*, Comedy Central's *Politically Incorrect*, and at least two magazines that no longer exist.

Geoff currently lives in New York City with his wife and three sons, none of whom bear any resemblance whatsoever to the characters in *The Tapper Twins Go to War (With Each Other)*.